HUNTED IN PARADISE

Examinations of Paradise
Book Four

JOHN HOLT

HUNTED IN PARADISE

Examinations of Paradise
Book Four

ABSOLUTELY AMAZING eBOOKS

For Ginny

When you give a hungry man a license
To do most whatever that he please
He'll lead you to the point of desperation
And then he'll want to drive you to your
knees

She said "Drive On, Driver"
by Danny O'Keefe

HUNTED IN PARADISE

Examinations of Paradise
Book Four

-ONE-

NONE OF THIS EVER ENDED. *Each step took forever, seconds expanding beyond mundane linear time. Far away he saw a car's headlights flash between two buildings. He wanted to be there. Out in the middle of the street screaming that he was alive – maybe even partially sane, but he was far from that point, a place he imagined offered salvation, an escape from the craziness, the wild, motionless madness he was trapped in now. Forever, that's how long he'd been trying to get there to the street and still, after a million years, he was no closer – the Buddhism kalpa rag in shoddy regalia. He was right in the middle of this one relentless, never-changing spot. Where he'd always been. Why was this going down? Well past reason; and why were there snakes squirming and coiling in his head – nuclear bright images of the reds, blacks and damn virginal whites of the milk snake, and those threatening dead moss greens and browns of the rattlesnake? The reptiles flickered in his mind, probing places without memory but filled with pain. Dead cold eyes sliced up his soul. He shivered. He didn't understand anything.*

Goddamnit! Had his life always been this way? He tried to remember another time, another reality ... another place. What did mountains look like? Or the high plains? Forests? Rivers? Cutthroat trout? People he knew? He could not conjure up any familiar faces of friends or even enemies to reassure him, to let him know that once he'd been alive. No woman's embrace with her warm sweet breath or gentle whisperings. Nothing. Not one thing came to him other than the awareness that women may have once existed for him, and perhaps other aspects of life had once been tangible, too. All there was now was this cold, miasmic, claustrophobic alley with the backsides of decaying red brick buildings, decrepit structures that slid in and out of sight as an icy winter fog swirled thick and rank in a raging wind that howled in the wires overhead. Downdrafts of iced air whipped around his feverish head. Water dripping from rusted drainpipes sounded mushy in the darkness. Feeble light from lamps bolted to leaning, rotting wooden poles threw a pale, yellow glow down onto the wet pavement. The reflections were weak, lifeless. Shadows cast by trash bins and neglected parked cars slithered away into dark corners of the scene. He looked around his feet and could not see his shadow. Was he dead? He thought he felt that way. But then, his lungs did burn from thousands of cigarettes he'd sucked down one after the other, and his soul ached for a drink. He could feel pain and that was something to hold on to. The putrid smell of uncollected garbage gagged him.

Would this insanity ever end? The snakes said no as they slithered and hissed inside him.

"This is hell," he muttered as he lit another Camel. He exhaled and the smoke became the fog that closed in. Looking behind him and then up ahead he realized that he was still below an old apartment building. He was going nowhere. All of it was the same. Always the same. And he forever felt like he was being stalked. The back of his head tingled with that fear, but there was never anyone when he turned around. No dark menacing silhouettes. Being robbed and murdered

would be a relief. An end.

Dim light oozed from a pair of open windows three floors above. "He's a woman, she's a man." Mournful music drifting out of those windows, the musician's whiskey-gravel voice dampened by the fog. He was unable to see anyone moving inside, drinking a beer, eating a sandwich, smoking a cigar or peering down at him. "This is hopeless," he thought. He looked around one more time. He was sweating, even in the light rain and snow, and he was walking as fast as he could, but he was still in the same place. The cracked and chipped bricks, the chilled concrete beneath him, the windows, the cars, the trash, the fog, the music – "Take your partner by the hand, he's a woman, she's a man, what's so hard to understand." Panic ripped through him. Over and over and over this went. He was beat, exhausted. The snakes, the words, the repetition, the going nowhere. He could not get rid of any of it. All the same. Nothing changed. He was used to this part of things and he hated what there was of his life, which wasn't much, while at the same time this stagnant setting was more than he could take. He rode the terrifying rush of the realization that things would be this way for eternity, heart racing, eyes wide open and bulging. And when the horror subsided as it always did like waves of alcohol withdraw tremors, nothing was any different than before. Only the surety that everything would keep circling in the same way, even the snakes. This was the point in the cycle where they crawled out of his head and wrapped themselves around his neck, his chest, his legs. They were all over the alley as far as he could see. Milk snakes and rattlesnakes, and now gopher and garter snakes. For some reason he could remember what they should look like, what they were called. All of them felt colder than this winter night as they squeezed hard against him. Rattles buzzed like wasps on Quaaludes. Thousands of gaping mouths hissed at him. The sound was a suggestive roar, a black river washing him away to darker places. The noise overpowered the music leaking out the window above. One long, thick rattlesnake glided out from the shadows and began climbing up his leg. Other snakes dropped to the ground to make way for this one. The pressure of the animal's muscles rippled in a nightmare rhythm. Razor-sharp fangs glinted in the dull light. Snake eyes sizzled in hellish recognition.

He started to run. Again.

~ ~ ~

The band of antelope was standing on a rocky hill a couple of hundred yards upwind of Jack. The pronghorn does grazed on the fresh grass that burst through the moist ground of late April. They would look up from their feeding, glance around and scan the horizon for any sign of danger, then drop their tan-and-white, black-masked heads back down and resume eating. They were wary animals that would, if alarmed, run with the wind and disappear over the ridge in seconds. A big buck lay just below the crest of the hill soaking in the warmth of the spring sun. His dark eyes looked down on his harem. "With satisfaction," thought Jack as he observed the animal through the crosshairs of the riflescope from his cover behind a clump of scruffy junipers. The smell of the bushes reminded him of gin, maybe with a splash of tonic, and he smiled at the inanity of the thought. The 3x9 scope pulled the animal right up to him. Jack watched as the buck blinked away mosquitoes buzzing about his head and moist nose. "Sometimes I feel like I'm being watched from behind through a riflescope," and he wondered at the origin of the notion, before pushing the thought from his mind and zeroing in on a spot along the antelope's neck. He slowly sucked in a large breath and squeezed the trigger. The well-worn .243 cracked sharply. The buck's head jerked back, then forward. The animal rolled over and downhill before slamming against a rusty-red outcropping of clinker. It was dead. Jack never missed. By the time he lowered the rifle, a space of only a few seconds, the females were out of sight, long gone over the far ridge and probably high-tailing it up brushy Mad Woman Gulch and then out onto the miles of tall grass, wide open bench land that rolled off towards the Sanders Mountains rising purple then late-winter white miles away down in Wyoming. Jack stood up, stretched, and side-hilled his way to the antelope. Blood oozed from a wound in the broken neck and soaked the grass, coloring both it and the salmon-tinted earth a moist brown. He grabbed buck's horns and pulled the animal's head down between his legs, then slit its throat to bleed the pronghorn.

He was almost out of meat. Only some mule deer pot roasts, a few pounds of catfish fillets and a couple of rounds of smoked black bear sausage remained, And, besides, he wanted fresh meat. He had a taste for it right now. The idea of waiting until the autumn hunting season didn't register in his mind. He'd let the antelope hang and age for a while but he'd fry up its liver in a cast-iron skillet tonight.

Graves had lived in this harsh, dry country that lay well away from cities like Billings, Miles City and Casper, land that had little to offer the well-moneyed tourists and developers that were destroying the best of the West with their greed and rapacious self-absorption. Very little sparkling water for trout streams and no spectacular Rocky Mountain vistas or plush ski resorts to call in the babbling hordes of pathetically over-dressed California or East Coast yuppies burdened with iPads and an insatiable lust for money. Just dry, dusty, brutally cold in the winter and oven-hot in the summer, unspoiled country full of snakes, sage, cactus, poisonous spiders, flies, ticks and never-ending skies filled with riotous amalgamations of clouds, stars, meteors, northern lights and a whole bunch of stuff he never even tried to explain to himself or anybody else. He'd lived in this place all his life, close to fifty years – was born prematurely in the back of a banged-up black 1958 Ford pickup as his dad frantically drove like a bat out of northern high plains hell on bald tires along narrow dirt two-tracks, sliding all over the place in the thick, Workman Plateau dust, or banking off slight berms of soil and rock along the sides of the road, or flying through the air as the old truck leaped over frost-heaved bulges along the way and then came crashing back to earth in a wrenching cacophony of severely stressed metal, Graves' mother lying on dirty mounds of hay left from feeding their few cattle earlier in the day, her screams as she pushed the child from her womb through the torn opening between her legs and out onto the now bloody hay, those screams ripping through the pines and slicing cleanly across the clear air.. By the time they reached the hospital in Drew, a two-hour run, Jack was already wrapped in an old Hudson Bay blanket, clutched tightly in his mother's arms and suckling hungrily on one of her breasts. That's how he came into this life, and the rest of the way, the past fifty years or so, had been pretty much free form and unpredictable.

No one around here worried about hunting regulations. He never had nor had his father or grandfather. Certainly not his great-grandfather who homesteaded this wind-swept, undisciplined country more than a hundred years ago, back when not many people came this way and even fewer stayed around.

When they needed meat they went out and shot it. Whenever, at any time of the year. There was plenty of game in this country if you knew where to look and how to move with the land and within its subtle rhythms of coulee, bluff, cliff, hill, wind and water. Antelope, mule deer, whitetail, even the occasional elk and black bear roamed the land, as did large numbers of Sage and Sharp-tailed grouse, and Merriam's turkeys.

Only this morning Jack killed one of the big birds, a twenty-five pounder with nearly a foot-long dirty black beard growing out of its chest – a sure indication of an old turkey. He'd shot it in the head with his Savage .22-20-gauge after it first dropped down from its roost tree, a huge Ponderosa pine that had been hammered by lightning strikes more times than he could remember, the tree's top a cluster of shattered, blasted limbs.

This country was dominated by open stands of the massive trees. The dead, long, brown needles carpeted the ground. Even the merest touch of breeze set up a lonesome moan through the big pines' branches. Large, sharp-edged cones lay in piles beneath them. Graves had spent many nights sitting around warm fires tossing in hundreds of them one after another, watching as they burst into flame, the red and orange sparks exploding up into the night and sailing away, winking out one by one, sometimes many feet above the fire.

Twenty, maybe thirty of the birds slept in the battered Ponderosa. As the dawn light came on over the country, the purest of light blues shading into the star-filled purple-black of retreating night, he watched as the turkeys awoke, dropped to the ground, and then clumsily shook themselves to organize their feathers and perhaps to rattle some semblance of consciousness into their wild, goofy bird brains. He picked out a large male from among the smaller jakes. The big boy was kicking up grass and dirt with his feet. He constantly shook his thick feathers and stretched and waggled his ungainly neck, the ugly red wattles making a queer sight. "Almost obscene," thought Jack. He chose the older bird with its tougher meat because his woman friend was always impressed with how tender the flesh was when he finished cooking it. She always exclaimed, "Jack, this is so damn good. I love the way you do meat." She always said this and he always liked hearing it. When he shot the turkey through the head, the others went running off "puttering" and "clucking" in a terrible racket. They could move as fast as racehorses and were long gone by the time he crawled out of his hiding place among a pell-mell pile of crumbling sandstone.

The horizon glowed silver at the approach of the sun. A lone coyote howled from a bluff a mile south. Then a band to the east picked up the riff and added a note of its own at the end, the animals' chattering and howling rising in pitch right to the end of the measure. The last cry reminded him of something Ornette Coleman had written – *Lonely Woman*. A measure played in his head. The lone coyote seemed to pick up on the tune, extending the music and leaving it open-ended for the others, who took off from there. This went on with serious, new-day enthusiasm for a few minutes and by the time the coyotes finished they had a pretty good little jazz melody going. "Better than Coleman himself," thought Jack. He liked the way the coyotes talked. They sounded like the land looked to him. Free. Lonesome. No rules. Hunting out here alone, this was how he lived. Where he lived. What he lived for. And he'd done that this morning – risen in the dark, dropped down a dry wash of limestone that lay before him like giant stairs leading to some ancient and now vanished monument. Then he'd scrambled up the side of a slope of loose yellow and grey rock, and climbed across a thick seam of exposed coal before moving silently among the substantial, dark shapes of the Ponderosas that rose silently skyward, walked to his hiding place where he pushed back in against the cold rock and then waited to kill the turkey.

The bird's carcass was now hanging, nailed by the feet, to the shed behind his place. A couple of days of aging plus three more marinating in a mixture of orange, pineapple and apple juice along with Worcestershire Sauce, freshly-ground black pepper and garlic would do the trick. Then he'd call Natalie and ask her over for dinner. She liked the way he grilled the turkeys over white-hot coals and a closed lid for an hour or so. When the bird was cooked, its skin fired a rich brown, Jack would lift it from the grill, drop the browned flesh on a large wooden cutting board, slice the meat into large, juicy chunks and bring it to the round cedar table near the wood stove in his kitchen. They'd eat like wolves, ripping and tearing at the meat and they'd devour huge Idaho bakers buried in butter and sour cream. Gnawed bones lay scattered everywhere. Grease and meat juices ran down their chins and forearms. And they'd knock down a half-dozen or so bottles of red wine, maybe some Californian Merlot if that's what turned Natalie on that night, or maybe they'd work on a bottle of two of Jim Beam poured over ice in big glass tumblers. "Adult highballs," she called these. He preferred the whiskey, but he also liked to get laid, so if she wanted the wine, he gave her what she wanted. He'd picked up a few cases of the Merlot from a tiny winery in the Sonoma Valley three years ago while back there visiting a gunsmith who did excellent work. The wine, the meat, the whiskey, all of it was a game and they both knew it.

His submissiveness for hers later on. They were both into it and the ancient ritual gave them each a good deal of pleasure. Once or twice a week this happened. Had been going on for several years.

He cut off the antelope's head and gutted the animal. The blood on his hands and forearms dried quickly in the warm midday breeze. He wasn't interested in trophies to hang on the flat-cut log walls of his cabin or above the mantle of the fireplace. The horns on this buck were close to sixteen inches. Trophy horns by most standards. But he only wanted the meat and that was that. The remains fed the turkey vultures, ants and coyotes. He lifted the carcass up and slung it over his shoulders. A hundred pounds at the most. He was a few inches over six feet, weighed maybe one-eighty and could walk all day through this country. The two-mile carry to home was nothing. On the way back as he skirted some more protrusions of clinker, he spotted a western terrestrial garter snake just before it slid into a dark crevice. The thing looked like a rattlesnake but was harmless. "Chickenshit," he said to the rocks and walked on. Back at the shed he strung the antelope by its hind legs with some soft hemp rope looped over a beam, looked across the miles of grass, sage, and blazes of wildflowers, grinned at the insane beauty, then went inside to make some coffee.

~ ~ ~

A few days later Jack and Natalie finished off the turkey, as always grilled perfectly, washed up and headed out to the front porch for postprandial conversation. The night was early-spring warm, the air rich with the smell of new growth, of fresh grasses, the warming soil, and the budding leaves that were popping out on the bright, red-skinned alders, and willows that grew thickly along a small spring-fed creek bubbling away in a small cut in the hills nearby. Small brown trout, real small, darted about beneath the brushy overhangs and along the sandy streambed that was flecked with pieces of fossils he could never identify. The browns came from a hatchery up north. Natalie used to work as a fisheries biologist with the Montana Department of Fish, Wildlife and Parks, but ten years of bureaucratic nonsense, backstabbing and career protecting at the expense of the fish and the rivers proved to be more than enough for her. Thoroughly outspoken during her tenure with the department, her determination to do what was right by the fish won her some admirers among her colleagues, and quite a few determined enemies. So when Jack mentioned the idea of stocking browns she called a friend at the Lewistown hatchery and was informed that the boys up that way were experimenting with a "hyper-strain" of browns from Scotland, one that readily adapted its growth and feeding habits to the size and food sources of a given stretch of water. After explaining what Jack had in mind, the biologist was more than happy to part with a few of his "*piscatorial wunderkinder.*" She told Jack and he raced up there to pick up two hundred of the fry. So small they looked black like minnows. He'd hauled them back in a Coleman cooler with a battery-run fish tank oxygenator and then dumped them in his place. Only a few had died from the trauma of the trip and the splashy introduction to his stream. The remainder had survived and grown in number over the past six years, spreading throughout the crooked miles of the creek all the way down to the main river. They never grew larger than five or six inches. Dark brown, covered in spots of jet black and flaming crimson with golden bellies. In the fall the down-sized males developed hooked lower jaws and humped backs, just like their much larger relatives swimming away in the state's famous trout streams. A couple of times each year he'd crawl on hands and knees up to the creek with 4-foot-four inch Orvis bamboo Banty fly rod his father had given him years ago and he'd dap a small grey dry fly, nothing more than a wisp of elk hair, some grey dubbing and a grizzly hackle. The tiny pattern would ride high in the current where it slipped under the willows or would spin round and round on the edges of bucket-sized eddies. The miniature browns would race out from the shade, slam the fly and then whirl about in diminishing circles until he would pull the fish to him and wiggle them free of the barbless hook. This brought him more pleasure than hunting the two-foot browns of the Yellowstone or Way over-fished Missouri. This world was everything a trout stream could be only condensed to a crystal-sharp intensity that thrilled him more than the raging pull of a five-pound trout ever did. The clear, cool water, the colorful rocks and sand, the protective cover of bush and grass and those wild little brown trout – he couldn't explain the fascination and really never even tried to anymore. All he could ever say to Natalie was "Damn yuppies won't float this baby," and she'd laugh at the expression of his deep anger mixed with irony and a touch of self-deprecation.

They sat down in two weathered wicker chairs. Jack lit Natalie's cigarette for her and did the same for his large Cuban H. Upmann cigar. A bottle of Beam stood between them on a small table along with two glasses holding and inch or so of the amber whiskey. The heavens were turning on as darkness settled in. Jupiter was rising in the east looking like the landing lights of a 747, growing brighter as it climbed above the horizon, so much so that the planet actually looked like an aircraft coming towards them. The sky still glowed a soft, deepening, and at once fading, orange far to the southwest over the dark shapes of the towering

Sanders Mountains rising down in Wyoming. Above the porch hundreds of stars and distant galaxies dotted the sky. Soon there'd be thousands, then God only knew how many. Enough to make your eyes cross and your brain go dead. The land, the evening breeze, everything, hummed with the just-barely-subtle energy of spring exploding across the plateau. The northern high plains, country that looked so dead and lifeless in its dirty browns and dusty cover of old snow only a month ago, was coming alive in a hurry. Life flashed everywhere. Nighthawks boomed and hooted. Bats swooped right in front of their faces as the mammals fed on midges buzzing in the air. Kingbirds, meadowlarks, robins, swallows, and other small birds chirped and chattered in the dark, damn glad to be alive and unable to contain themselves. The birds would go silent sometime after midnight and start all of this again well before sunrise.

Natalie looked over at Jack and marveled again at how much he reminded her of her long-dead father. From the profile to the build, the voice, the way both men looked at a problem from all angles, decided on a course of action, then took it. 'Yes, Jack and my father are the same man in so many ways. Why do we always want to sleep with our fathers,' and this thought both saddened and excited her.

"We made it through another one, girl," and they clinked glasses and laughed at the absurdity of taking the wintertime struggle seriously and then they shared a look, eyes sparkling in the night, a look about what happened between them earlier today alongside the dusty road that snaked through the emerald hills between her place and his.

They were driving down the road, the truck kicking up red dust that the warm afternoon wind swept out over the vast sage flats. Rounding a ninety-degree turn they pulled over next to an old grave that looked out upon the far-ranging openness that was partially defined by a series of small valleys, nothing more really than eroded slices in the Workman plateau. The cuts were filled with stands of Ponderosa and juniper. A bunch of antelope jumped up from a near hillside and bounded away, rump hair flaring, down a narrow draw and away from view. The gravesite was nearly seventy years old. On the tombstone was written *"April 23, 1950 – Here lies Wimpy Quinn. A good, honest man and my friend. The damn bank took all his money, so he drank himself to death." His angry wife.* The area was garishly decorated with clumps of plastic flowers – weather and time faded = red roses; black-eyed Susans; purple, white and orange tulips, and lots of carnations. Hundreds of them. A pile of empty whiskey bottles was mounded along where Jack and Natalie imagined the body was buried. Four worn-out tires completed the arrangement which was enclosed with four strands of rusted barbed wire nailed to gnarled pine stakes. Aluminum pie pans were hammered along the length of each post. An old fire pit surrounded by large stones was off to one side. Two rusted breaker bars lay in the middle, barely visible through the silvery-green sage now growing there.

Jack plucked a brace of cold Raniers from a cooler, the one that had held the tiny browns, in the bed of the truck and popped them both open with a whoosh and lots of foam.

"Ever know the Quinns?" she asked, as she took her beer from Jack and had a long drink. "Heard they had quite an operation during World War II. A beef contract with the army or something."

"Dad was good friends with Wimp. Used to hunt and trap with him. Mink, otter, beaver, raccoon, jackrabbit, red fox. Even a couple of badgers. Pelts are those hanging on my bedroom wall. They helped each other out when one of them needed a hand, which, from what Dad said, was most all of the time for both of them," said Jack as he pulled two more beers from the ice. "Steers knocking down fences, irrigation ditches clogged, machinery broken down, pipes frozen, half the roof blown away in a winter gale. Quinns homesteaded 'bout the same time as my family. Before the turn of the century. Came out from southern Wisconsin same as we did. Irish. Whenever he talked about Wimp, and he loved the guy, he'd always end whatever story he was telling about the two of them together with "Avoid the Irish," and then he'd break up and actually roll on the floor with laughter. From what I heard, I could see why, but those stories aren't for the faint of heart."

"Jack, come on. Tell me some," Natalie pleaded. "Haven't I been nice to you lately," and she hugged him and pushed hard against him with her hips then moved quickly away with a charming 'How can you resist this' smile. All five-foot-eight of her comely shape moved suggestively as she ran her hands through her thick head of red hair.

"God, Natalie. You've got so many damn speeds I never know what's going on in your head. Maybe after dinner tonight." She smiled and held his gaze briefly before looking down at her feet. Jesus! She always gets her way. Makes me like doing things I don't like. Things I would never think of doing. Like dancing or listening to classical music. Debussy over morning coffee. Waltzing on the porch at night. Where do I start and you end? Can't ever win with you, so why even try. Screw it. He kicked some dust into the breeze. Then he wondered about the age something men always seem to wonder about and had to ask her.

"Are you seeing anyone else? We've been doing

whatever it is we're doing for so long, I just had to ask. Sorry."

"Heavens no. Just keeping up with you keeps me occupied full-time aside from my work," and she sent him a demure smile. "If I were, I'd tell you. I promise."

And he said, "Okay," and he believed her, but had lost his train of thought, and she picked up on that and prompted him.

"So tell me, what happened next with Quinn? Avoid the Irish and then what?"

"After the war the contract ended, Wimp came up well short money-wise two years running. He'd expanded too much – new barn, too many cattle, new appliances for Adell. Wimp never saw the end of that fat run with the government coming. Dry years hammered his grass and that was that. Bank called in his loans. He would have been forced to move out, but instead decided to slam the booze. Must have of smoked three-hundred cigarettes a day, too."

Jack looked at several empty whiskey bottles of his own lying in the back of the old pickup. He pulled a gold-plated Zippo lighter from his pocket and bummed a Newport from Natalie. After lighting the smoke he stared at the figure of a snake etched into the lighter's well-worn, soft finish. The reptile was a composite of square and triangular shapes with two mad oval eyes on top of its flat head and a grotesque curving tongue. His father, Jack Senior, or Senor as Wimp called him, picked it up for a handful of ragged pesos while in Mexico City. Bought it from an old drunk who desperately needed a drink, a lot of drinks, while he and Wimp killed off a night hanging out in a dingy cantina fifty years ago, gave it to him on his twentieth birthday, saying 'Light your cigs with this. You'll never quit until they pound the last nail into your coffin, anyway. Happy birthday.' His Dad was like that. Covering up his soft side with harsh talk. He and Wimp had driven down that way in an old Ford truck loaded to the gills with camping gear and a few rifles in search of the near mythical onza cat. They'd read an account of the cats in an old copy of *Unknown Mexico* written by an anthropologist named Carl Lumholtz back around 1900. One year after reading the book the two headed down south of the border to hunt panthers in the rugged, untraveled Sierra Madre Occidental country, a land sparsely inhabited by Indians and cutthroat bandits. Far back in a deep, unknown canyon surrounded by sheer, 8,000-foot rock walls, they came upon a band of Tarahumara, people who worshipped obscure gods with the aid of peyote, a reasonably strong hallucinogen. The Indians were open and friendly. The tribe asked the two with the simplest of sign gestures to join them for a feast that night which included drinking a fermented tea made from the drug. While dancing and whirling around a fire, Jack Senior flashed the gold Zippo. A Tarahumara snatched it from him and disappeared. Wimp and Jack Senior stayed up all night with the Indians. The next afternoon when he awoke, everything shimmering around the edges and looking a bit too real, he found the lighter sitting on top of his old Stetson. He noticed the engraving, the caricature of the snake sending shivers down his spine, and put it away in his pocket. The Tarhumara were gone. The village deserted, but both Jack and Wimp thought they could hear voices sounding like soft echoes floating around the place and drifting down from the canyon above them. Jack told his son that they'd followed the eerie voices that seemed to be calling them deeper and deeper into the surreal land for several days. They lived on enormous gold-colored trout, some over thirty inches, that they snagged with a short casting rod, treble hooks and lead weight they'd brought along. 'Biggest damn trout I'd ever seen,' said his father. Wading up the canyon through the middle of the cool stream, praying that it wouldn't rain and wash them away in a flash flood, they stumbled upon the tracks of an enormous panther. Tracks that pressed deep into the reddish sand. Four toes per print measuring eight inches front to back, the paired prints several feet apart and leading to a sheer wall. A few miles further the voices were replaced with an unearthly howling that roared down at them and ricocheted off the sheer cliffs. The noise grew closer, deafening. Then the largest cat either of them had ever seen, an animal that dwarfed the 120-pound mountain lions of Montana, appeared on top of a large boulder, vicious teeth glinting and deep tan fur shining in the orange light reflecting off the walls. The cat's menacing yellow eyes were the size of plums. Later they estimated the panther at somewhere between 250 and 300 pounds. Both men raised their guns and prepared to shoot, but the cat crouched, leapt and soared over their heads. They could smell its fetid breath, reeking of digesting flesh, as it sailed by. Before they could swing on the animal, it was gone. That's all his father ever told him of that trip, except to remark that those days in the canyon altered his way of looking at things. As for the lighter he would only say when asked 'They must have known that we have a lot of snakes up here in Montana.' Following his return from Mexico, Jack Senior was taciturn where once he'd been almost ebullient. He still carried himself erectly but he appeared humbled, not proud to the point of arrogance as he'd been in the past. His mother, Ernie and area ranchers noticed the change, but as time passed they forgot the old Jack Senior and acted as though he'd always been this way. Jack put the lighter away, took a drag from the cigarette and resumed his tale.

"Dad tried to help Adell, Wimp's wife, sober him up, but coming off the whiskey damn near killed him. Shakes. Convulsions. Hallucinating gigantic Angus bulls right in their kitchen stomping the old Monarch stove to pieces and punching holes through the floorboards. And so on. A real zoo filled with stuff that wasn't there. The second time according to Dad, Wimp said "Fuck this shit," staggered out to the shed where he kept a stash of whiskey and was dead in four days. Found him slumped over the wheel of his old Packard. Coroner said his heart gave out and his liver was close behind. Adell, Dad and Mom, just about everyone else around the area buried Wimp right here. Took them half the day to dig through the rock and hard-packed dirt. Dad built the coffin out of cured slabs of Ponderosa he was saving to make a dining room table. Lowered the casket into the hole with chains. Each person said a few words. Adell, smiling and crying at the same time, closed with "I'll see you again, Wimp." After the ceremony they drank themselves silly all night and most of the next day. Built a huge fire and roasted a couple of antelope over it. Right in that pit," and Jack pointed a rough, tanned forefinger in the direction of the circle of rocks and then ran the hand through his thinning brown hair. "Elmer Yoter disappeared with his 30.06 early in the proceedings and put the sneak on some does. There weren't nearly as many of them back then. They were bound for extinction until Teddy Roosevelt and others stepped in. Numbers have grown over the decades. Now you see them all over the place. Elmer must have dragged the gutted animals for miles. No one at the wake heard the rifle shots. When he returned he was covered with blood, dirt and prickly pear needles. In those days he was six-ten and weighed over 300 pounds. He's shrunk some since."

"I just saw him driving around in that wreck of truck with all his dogs," Natalie said. "Barking and howling. What a racket."

"Yeah he loves those ridiculous Boykin spaniels. Bought four of them from some loony plantation owner in South Carolina. Claims they're the best bird dogs he's ever seen. Boykins. Even the name makes me laugh," said Jack between sips of beer. "Curly brown nitwits. Make the Springers I used to have look tame and they went wire to wire twenty-four hours a day."

"I meant Elmer," Natalie laughed and so did Jack. "Head out the window yodeling some crazed cowboy lament. Something about 'Cool clear water.' That mangy hat of his with the milk snake skin band hanging on by a thread. Red-faced. Not something you see all the time and those dogs. Howling along with him."

"Always the four oldest dogs up front and the rest, eleven or twelve last I saw, howling and running around on the flatbed," he said. "Drives all day with them, rain or shine, summer or winter, drinking Pabst beer and Kessler's whiskey. Fixed that muffler, yet?"

"No. I could hear the damn thing coming for miles," she said. "And the clouds of exhaust. God, what a sight. I'm amazed the politically correct fools haven't tried to ban his rig."

"Guy's at least eighty and never did like ranching, all the work. Mending fence, repairing busted machinery, feeding. Any of it," said Jack after bumming another cigarette from her. Inhaling, he paused then said through a cloud of smoke "God, these things are awful," and Natalie laughed and told him to smoke his own. "I'm out. These will do. As for Elmer, he's got more money than the rest of us put together. He scored big on some oil leases recently, and sold the mineral rights to the coal under his land years ago. Dark Star Consortium owns the rights now and I heard talk in town the other day at The Mint that they're thinking of surveying the land in preparation for strip-mining. And they're trying to revive plans to put a rail line along the Workman between Drew and Miles City. Anything to save a few bucks hauling the coal. Say good-bye to another chunk of this place ... but..." and Jack looked over a rise to the northeast and off into Dolphy River Country..." they might want to get to the stuff soon. A century ago lightning struck some exposed seams and that coal's been simmering away all this time. The ground above is hot, even through my boots. On calm days you can see whiffs of smoke coming through cracks in the cooked soil. Looks like Yellowstone Park on his place, except without the water, or the tourists. Only things growing there are some scrub sage, withered cactus and thistle. Cattle won't touch those sections. Neither will the game. February snow won't even stick to it.

"Do you still have those rights to your land, Jack?" she asked.

"Yeah. I asked Dad about that a long time ago, just before he died and he said he'd never sell a single part of the place including what lay beneath it," said Jack. "Dad always played it straight with me. Never lied about a thing. Signed the place over to me in his will, since Mom had died of brain cancer when I was about thirty," and he looked away and his eyes moistened. "Sorry. Still can't deal with that. Ate her alive and caused her more pain than I've ever seen one person go through in my life," and he caught his breath choking back the emotion of all of it before proceeding.

"Hell, at any rate, by the time they'd cleaned and skinned the does and stuck them on a couple of breaker bars over the fire, old Elmer was pretty well shit-hammered, dancing around while Coaker Triplett played the Garryowen, Custer's marching song, on his fiddle. Man's still good. Puts Vassar Clements to shame. Elmer started leaping over the edge of the coals and eventually fell in. Dad and Coaker rolled him out of there and Elmer was fine. Wool shirt was singed a bit, though. Hung it on a wall near his fireplace and it's still there. Goofy bastard," He looked over by the gravesite to the fire pit and imagined he could see Elmer lying smoldering in the fire beneath the roasting antelope, juice from the cooking meat dripping on him and splattering on the white-hot coals, imagined he could hear the shrill notes of Coaker's fiddle and imagined he could see his parents and their friends dancing and laughing around the blaze in the middle of that late-April night so many years ago. He turned away. "The rest of the wake was more of the same – drinking, dancing, bullshitting, and a little romance off in the dark. Sounds like a great time all things considered.

"The tires are from Wimp's Packard. Dad and a couple of friends pulled them off before they'd let the bank's repo man haul the car away. Shotguns and tire wrenches work every time. Wimp used to hunt out of that car. Threw the dead animals in the back seat. Dried blood all over the carpet and seats. Dog and deer hair as thick as a rug. Quite a rig. He'd cut a hole in the roof over the front seat. Used a hammer, file and hacksaw, then rigged a canvas tarp over it. Probably the first sunroof in Montana," and he smiled at the vision. "They never had any kids. Ran the whole damn place themselves. So after the wake Adell moved back to Clinton, Wisconsin and lived with her brother's family on a dairy farm out there. She came back about twenty years ago. Stayed at my place for a few days. That's when she added the flowers and pie plates for what reason no one knows, and that's it."

"Life can be tough here, can't it, Jack. The work,

the weather and the drinking," said Natalie. Her eyes wandered out over the land. "Keep things small like you do and live modest. The hell with lots of money. Screw it. Right, Jack? Seems to work for you."

He looked hard at her and she returned the stare. 'Screw it' she said. Reading my mind again. No peace in the valley for this boy.

"Hundred damn cows, give or take, brings in enough for fuel, food, utilities, odds and ends. Place is paid for and I don't need much in the way of things. I've got all I want," and his gaze followed her line-of-sight. This country is plenty. All I could hope for, he thought, and before he could say it, Natalie turned to him and blurted "And of course there's that outrageous blue-ribbon trout stream of yours," and that was it. They fell into each other's arms, laughing and yelling something about McKenzie drift boats and Spey rods.

Then they began to kiss, passionately, fondling each other, but Jack pulled away and looked around for any approaching vehicles. Some of the roads went for days without use and then it was usually a rancher headed into town or off to visit a neighbor and there were the black trucks of the coal company's survey crews, side panels emblazoned *Dark Star Consortium, Vehicle ID #1666* or whatever.

"Not here, Natalie. Anyone could drive by."

"Why not?" she asked as she dropped to her knees and worked on his belt and zipper. "Now, not later."

"No girl. Not now." He made a weak attempt at stepping back, but she persisted, hands everywhere.

Jack gave in to another of his hungers. He never could control or resist any of them for very long – sex, hunting, lots of good food, whiskey. He leaned back on the truck's tailgate, looked down at Natalie, pushed his hands into her hair and pulled her head to him. He looked off towards the Sanders Mountains, then he didn't see anything.

By then she had his jeans down around his ankles and had shed her cowboy boots and Levis. She pushed up against him and guided him in with her hands. Both of them were rocking and moaning, lost to the world, when out of the blue in a cloud of exhaust and thick dust Elmer and his pack of disturbed Boykins roared around the corner and into view, the old man's flushed red face, topped by that filthy hat, leaning far out the window, largemouth filled with stained teeth, tongue flapping away.

"I'm an old cowhand from the Rio Grande..." Elmer's voice screeched and hacked above the roar of the mufflerless engine, sixteen spaniels howling and yapping along to the tune. Thirty-four eyes, some of them not yellowed and blood-shot, took in the action with carefree, maniacal delight. Seventeen tongues drooled in the wind. Jack and Natalie looked up from what they were doing, up at the insane sight of Elmer and all those dogs. Both of them stunned and embarrassed at best.

Elmer and his crew never missed a beat or an awkward note. Thundering past the two love makers, the dogs wagged their tails. Elmer tipped his hat, smiled and tossed a full can of Pabst in their direction. The beer exploded on impact and rolled to their feet, shooting its foamy contents all over them. By then the chartreuse GMC flatbed was out of sight, backfires, awful singing and god-awful yowling trailing in a wake behind the menagerie.

Jack looked down at their soaked feet and ankles and said, "At least something came. I sure as hell can't now. Probably never will again." They looked up from the beer into each other's eyes and howled themselves. Bare-ass naked they hopped and leapt around the over-grown fire pit until Jack tripped over the pants around his boots and fell into the middle of it pulling Natalie on top of him.

"God, we're as bad as Elmer was all those years ago, but at least he had his pants on," she yelled between sobs of laughter. "The more things change, the more they stay the same. Damn straight 'I'm an old cowhand from the Rio Grande'" she sang. They spasmed with laughter once again.

On the other side of the road a rattlesnake had been coiled on a flat piece of stone, nervously swinging its head about. Energy rippled along its muscular length. It began forcing its head against a rough rock breaking loose the layer of dead skin around its eyes. Then it loosened the skin from around its jaws. Kinking and writhing its body, the snake worked the skin past its thick mid-section then pulled through the remaining part turning the shed skin into an inside-out, translucent replica of itself. It's new, bright scales glistened in the sun and the rattler slid away in a sidewinding motion, its skin rasping across the rock. The snake vanished into the dark shelter of a pile of jumbled sandstone, to hide for a while until its exterior toughened some. The Red-tailed hawk, uncommonly impassive throughout all of this uncommon behavior, lifted its wings, working them up and down with growing speed. The predator rose thirty feet above the road. Then it swooped down and snatched the shed skin in its talons and soared off on a late-afternoon thermal, riding the rising air up over the plateau towards the distant mountains.

The two of them saw none of this. They lay there together in each other's arms, eyes closed, beneath the hot sun for some time before getting up, pulling their pants on and heading on up the road to Jack's place.

He parked the truck in the shade by the house. They went in and made drinks. A little further on he poured some more whiskey in each of their glasses, took a long puff on his cigar and looked over to her. They both shook their heads. What could they say about any of it. The two of them bouncing away together, Elmer, the truck, all those dogs and the exploding can of beer. They looked off towards the eastern skyline.

The intense silver-white crescent of a new moon rose above the horizon casting shadows that ran black down the coulees. Ponderosa and sage threw long silhouettes across the land. Strange rock formations shone like quicksilver. Several coyotes barked in the excitement of recognizing the new, yet familiar, arrival in their sky. Suddenly, infinitely louder, a deep howl, rising up from the depths of an animal neither of them had ever heard before, washed across the plateau and ripped through Jack and Natalie's guts. It sounded like a creature from another world and another time. It wasn't from a coyote.

~ ~ ~

A pair of Dark Star trucks lurched over the rough ground on Elmer Yoter's ranch. The new rigs were painted glossy black with the company's logo, a bright yellow bolt of lightning along the doors, the words 'Dark Star Consortium' done in bright red beneath the yellow. The men in the trucks were out to begin surveying the land in preparation for strip-mining the coal sometime next year. Seismic studies of the fifty-odd sections of land holding the mineral had been completed two years ago. The four Dark Star employees had detailed maps showing where the seams of coal were, how far beneath the surface, how thick – exploratory drilling indicated that it was anywhere from twelve to thirty-seven feet and close to the surface, and where the seams ran. They had other maps showing how deep the ground water beneath the surface flowed and where it pooled into a large underground lake. Potentially the low-sulfur bituminous reserves could exceed a billion tons, enough to power the country for years. Dark Star had already reaped hundreds of millions of dollars from its holdings a few miles to the west over by McCoy, but these were beginning to play out and the company was preparing for the future. Trains pulling miles of cars were loaded with the black rock each day. Then they would haul their loads off to electrical generation plants at places like Colstrip and Gillette, Wyoming or more often, to the west coast for shipment to Pacific Rim countries. Power facilities with enormous appetites.

The mining left huge holes in the earth covering thousands of acres. All of the reclamation effort and technology in the world could not put the land back together again. Topsoil, tons of fertilizer and oceans of piped-in water temporarily turned some of the ravaged land into an artificially-green oasis, looking more like a cushy Palm Springs golf course than the high plains. The easily-duped eastern media bought the con, flashed stories of how low impact strip-mining was these days, a sustainable and environmentally benign source of energy that the country desperately needed; and of course the antelope and deer and elk loved the verdant grasslands, not to mention the piles of grain the company dumped all over the plastic scene. The phony place was a veritable delicatessen for the game, but most locals refused to hunt there saying something along the lines of "Like shooting deer at Disneyland." And once the company stopped spreading fertilizer and water on the soil, which they did as soon as the press lost interest in the story after about fifteen or twenty minutes, everything died, turned into a wasteland.

In the coming months the survey party would map

out the coal seams and haul roads to the proposed rail line along the Workman River. The line was expected to be ram-rodded through the Montana Legislature, a hodgepodge collection of mostly-bought-off political hacks. The line would be completed in as little as twelve months of blasting, grading and degradation to the river corridor. Spread some money, make some threats, a little blackmail, the usual stuff. Politicians came relatively cheap these days, as they always have.

The two trucks slowed as the terrain grew still more severe, distorted. The earth was faded shades of ochre and vermilion, jagged, heaved into abrupt hillocks that were fractured and broken into mangled pieces. The sky was a bleak, burning white. Even in spring this part of Yoter's ranch felt unnaturally hot on some days. A surreal vision of unmoving turmoil. Small clumps of desiccated sage and withered cactus dotted the landscape. Scattered about the lifeless landscape were groups of barren Ponderosa, thirty, forty foot skeletons of sun-bleached, grey wood, scraggly limbs thrust out like the arms of monstrous skeletons. Some of the trees, roots burned or rotted, had fallen over, and were lying on top of each other, trunks cracked, branches shattered. The juniper trees, thick and dark green with dusty-blue berries elsewhere on the plateau, were nothing but brittle sticks, emaciated to the point where the always-rushing wind found nothing to play with. Even in a gale the lifeless forms scarcely moved. Dead grey four-foot-tall stands of Russian thistle shuddered in the breeze like detoxing drunks. Recent spring rains had drenched the area. Still, this land was parched, baked bone-dry. Everywhere the men looked plumes of dirty white smoke issued from vents and narrow cracks in the nightmarish country.

"Goddamned place looks like hell," said a surveyor in one rig. "How in the name of Jesus can we haul our equipment in here? The fucking ground will collapse. And as soon as we open up the topsoil, the rush of oxygen will set some of these underground fires off like a bomb."

"Don't sweat it," said the driver, himself an engineer and geologist who'd worked this country for close to twenty years. "We'll pump enough water to put out Hiroshima. And the ground is hard enough to support our rigs. Held up okay when the test-drilling crews came out awhile back."

"Great plan, if you had the water," muttered the other, who was new to this part of the country. Appalachian destruction had been his beat up until this month.

"We do," and the driver pointed down Mad Woman Draw, a brushy defile that twisted and turned between Yoter's and Graves' place. "Owner of that land (pointing towards the Graves' property) has a spring on his land that's fed by a fair-sized aquifer. We'll tap that and pipe the water over this way. Run the line along the haul road from here over along the creek and down to the Workman when the new rail line is completed."

"Who owns the land and what if he won't sell the water?" asked the engineer as he lit a cheap cigar, blowing smoke that washed across the dusty dashboard and up the windshield. "Bastards out here hang on to what they've got most of the time. Damn land means more than money. Same as back east. Even when they're dead broke and starving. Surprised to beat shit that that old fuck Yoter sold his rights."

The driver laughed and said "Jack something, the owner over there," and he pointed up ahead to the just barely visible roof of the Jack's home behind a low rise, "doesn't know that his old man sold all the mineral rights for thirty-some-bucks an acre way back when to Northern High Plains Coal. Father took that little one with him to the grave. Guess who owns that? We do. Got a hold of NHPC in a hostile takeover when I first came out here. The old man got close to two-hundred grand, which was good money back in the fifties, 'specially for a run-down, drunk rancher. Story is, that the father never told his kid, too ashamed that he'd screwed his son over so bad. Probably the worst thing the guy ever did in his life. Heard he used the dough to pay off the place and set up a low-risk fund for the kid. We helped him bury the transfer so deep in legal bullshit in the contract that even some Harvard dip-shit lawyer couldn't figure it out, but our boys in the legal department can. Pulled things like this, greased the skids over the years, hundreds of times. Indians, ranchers, widows, hell, we'll fuck anyone," and the two laughed loudly, an ugly sound. "When we hit that sap with the news that we're going to tear hell out of his precious eleven sections, he'll get mad as hell. More than likely he'll wave around some guns. Losers like him usually do. Then we'll throw a little money his way for the water to quiet him down some and send his ass on its way out of here. What choice does he have? Play ball or disappear. His land will be nothing but a hole in the ground by the time we're done with it." The two in the truck exchanged a knowing look. Property rights and lives meant nothing to companies like Dark Star when billions of dollars were at stake. The cost of a hit on a man these days was only a few grand. Life was cheap. Coal was worth more than people to Dark Star.

"All of this looks the same to me. One piece of dry, worthless dirt pretty much like the next. Why here and not over there?" said the man from Appalachia pointing to a large sandstone cliff rising above a large, grassy bench in the distance.

The truck's driver looked at his companion and thought 'Why in the hell do they send me these dumb shits from back east? They don't know squat about the West,' but he tried to explain. "All of this is part of the Fort Union formation which breaks into three main sections – Tulluck, Lebo and Workman River, which is right here. The coal in these parts is largely folded under layers of sandstone that formed when an old sea dried up millions of years ago, and it's down pretty damn deep. We'll get to it when the price is right. For now we're taking the easy pickings near the top," and he looked out across Yoter's land and over to Jack' holdings. "Our geologists tell us there's over fifty billion tons in the region. Hell, we've got all the time in the world. We can out-wait and out-last these loser pricks forever. The people that live here are all either drunk or crazy or both. They cling for dear life to some lame romantic notion that this land is their heritage and their life. Fuck 'em. It's just dirt and rock. Without the coal and oil it would be worthless. Nothing but nothing. Get the picture?'

The other nodded and looked out the window seeing a shriveled carcass of a mule deer, skin drawn tight across the ribs, stomach torn open.

The driver checked the side mirrors to see where the other truck was. He slammed on the brakes. Five-hundred yards behind the front of the other black crew cab was axle deep in the ground. Smoke was billowing all around the rig and the two occupants were spraying fire extinguishers over the hood. The two in the first truck leaped out and ran back to their co-workers but by the time they reached the foundered truck, the machine was ablaze, all four tires burning and sending clouds of oily black smoke up and away across the cooking land. The four men backed away just before the burning truck's dual gas tanks exploded sending pieces of truck skyward and rocketing along at ground level. A chunk of door whistled towards them like a missile, slicing the eastern surveyor's legs cleanly just below the knees. The man tumbled backwards screaming, blood spurting from the stumps. Then a large ripping noise, like something was savagely pulling the earth apart, slammed through the air and the ground tore open at their feet. The whole place shook violently, heaving in all directions at once. The three who were not hurt instinctively fled for their lives forgetting all about their wounded co-worker. They ran, stumbled, crawled through and over cactus and unyielding iron-stiff sage limbs, getting back up and running from the expanding crack in the plateau, running until their lungs felt like they were going to explode. When they stopped, having out-distanced the tear in the cooked ground, they looked back. Geysers of smoke, flame and sparks were pouring into the air along a quarter-mile-long, wide gash. The roar of the released energy was deafening. Burning pieces of cactus and whole flaming sage plants were shooting hundreds of feet in the air before plummeting back to earth in a barrage of scorching stone and burning plants. The mangled man and the remains of the incinerated truck were gone.

Thousands of feet overhead five turkey vultures soared casually on six-foot wingspans describing large, lazy circles above the smoldering countryside.

~ ~ ~

Elmer pulled in front of Jack's place a little past noon. Natalie had left early for a fisheries management symposium in Billings. The scintillating affair was titled "Non-game fish introduction in state waters – Can we learn to live with it?" When she'd told him this, he just looked at her and walked over to the stove to pour another cup of coffee. He'd see her again in a week or so. Jack heard Elmer's truck coughing and farting its way up the road for the several minutes, but his dogs were strangely silent. No barks or howls. The four spaniels in the front were seated in an even row looking through the windshield. The twelve in the back were neatly arranged in two rows of six on each side of the flatbed.

"How they hangin', Jack old boy," Elmer yelled as he lurched down from the truck missing the running board and nearly falling on his face before executing a nifty three-sixty recovery, Pabst in one hand, cigar in the other. Even at eighty he was big. Six-eight and three-hundred at least. Old, faded blue jeans cinched by a thick leather belt below his big belly. Scuffed black cowboy boots and a huge washed-out green T-shirt with a pack of Muriel cigars in the pocket. A pint of Kessler's protruded from his hip pocket. Silver hair curled out beneath his old hat. "What's ya think of the damn dogs. Ever since they seen you and your girl goin' at it they ain't been the same."

"Thank god for that," cracked Jack as he snared a can of beer that Elmer winged his way. A pair of magpies went from tree to tree squawking heatedly about something. "Sorry about all that. We kind of got carried away there, in the heat of the moment."

"Sorry, my ass," boomed the old man. "Haven't seen a look like that on a man's face since I watched myself bouncing beneath a whore over in Wallace, Idaho fifty years ago. Had mirrors on the ceiling, the walls, everywhere. But back to my dogs. 'Bout five miles past your little go-round yesterday, they all went dumb on me. Haven't heard as much as a yip out of 'em since then. And this goddamned military drill team shit they're pulling now, well ... well I feel like shipping the whole bunch of 'em back to that cracker in South Carolina. Maybe they stand for that nonsense down there, but not this boy. No sirree Bob. No way in hell."

Elmer sounded mad, but Jack could see the

laughter dancing around the corners of his eyes. He watched as Elmer surveyed the troops. Not one of the Boykins so much as batted an eye, wagged a tail, shook a long, matted ear or licked its chops. Elmer looked the whole pile of them up and down for several minutes then turned to Jack with what seemed to resemble pride.

"Damn. Sure as hell never thought I'd live to see the day where this ragged-ass bunch of brown-haired mongrels shaped up like this," and he belched, broke wind and slurped his beer. "Most contrary bunch of hounds I ever laid eyes on. Look at 'em. Not one of their damn ears moves so much as an inch. Eyes don't even blink. Don't get me wrong here, I admire them northern Cheyenne just as much as the next fella, but I'll be goddamned if I'll have my dogs acting like they're members of those Indians' Contrary Society. A warring group like the Red Shields or the Elks is one thing, but this contrary business is another. Watch this!"

Elmer walked over and launched a playful jab at one dog's chest. Nothing more than a tap, really, but the Boykin never batted an eye and the other fifteen sat like marble statues, staring off into distant space.

"They think I don't know what they're up to, but I do. Smart little shits. Figure humans can do any damn thing they please, so why can't they. Like for instance, screwing by the side of a public road in plain view of decent folk such as myself," and Elmer cast a stern eye in Jack's direction, who at this point broke up laughing, spraying beer all over Elmer. "While we're at this, goddamnit, you're no better than these worthless, tick-ridden dogs," who were still lined up rock-still on the bed and in the truck. "They're trying' to break my spirit. That's what they're doin'. Figure they'll drive me nuts and I'll lose my marbles. Won't be able to keep up with them and then they'll be able to run the Sam hell all over the place," and he paused before turning on his canine tribe and pointed a huge, crooked forefinger at the Boykins.

"Guess again you lame pieces of cow crap. I ain't breaking'. So forget about it," and Elmer turned back to Jack who was still laughing. "Fuck you, too, boy. This is serious. Man's got to at least have the loyalty and respect of his dogs in this world or he's nothing'. Worse than nothin'. Hell, that's not why I'm here. Came over to tell ya what happened at my place yesterday just 'bout the time you and your lady friend were whooping it up."

Jack had known Elmer all his life, considered him one of his few friends. The man could talk a blue streak for hours and today clearly was going to be no exception, but before Elmer could start up again, Jack squeezed in a few words of his own.

"I wondered about those two Dark Star helicopters hovering over by Mad Woman this morning. Things make a tremendous racket, don't they? Vibrated the coffee cups off the kitchen table. What'd you do. Shoot one of their survey trucks, Elmer?"

"Didn't have to. Damn fools took care of that themselves without any help from me. Drove out there as pretty as you please without a care in the world," and he turned back to his dogs. "And they sure as hell did fine and damn-dandy without any help from you worthless beasts. God, look at 'em. Wish the hell they could hold a point like that when I'm out ground sluicing some thunder chickens."

"What the hell happened over there, anyway?" asked Jack who was looking past his friend's shoulder at the motionless dogs. "One of them drive into the gulch?"

"Not at all. Those coal seams been burning since as long as I can remember and one of Dark Star's rigs

35

broke through that hard pan. Thin as piecrust in spots. Shoulda had a man out front checking the ground," said Elmer as he pulled the pint out, drained a quarter of it and passed it to Jack who took a healthy slash himself and passed the bottle back. "Truck started burning' real good and that sucked air down onto the coal. Next thing you know, at least what they told me this morning 'cause I was over at Coaker's helping 'em fix that cheap-ass baler of his, the ground tore apart all to hell." Elmer laughed at the mere thought of the baler and probably the Dark Star fiasco, too.

"Truck's tanks exploded. Piece of door cut a man's legs off and then sucked both the truck and that poor bastard into the hole. Dumb shits. I told 'em that those sections out there weren't fit for humans, but did they listen to me. No way, pardnah. Now they're out a truck and an employee. Probably could give a shit 'bout the burned-up man, but they sure worked like hell pulling that truck out." Elmer spread his arms out, palms up as if in supplication, like why must he continue to suffer these fools brought his way.

"Watched the whole thing through my spotting scope. Hooked onto the wreckage with a grappling hook or something and those 'copters pulled it through the crack. What's left of it anyways. Fires gone down some, just smoke mainly. Their pickup looks shot to hell. Burnt to a crisp." Elmer took another pull on the whiskey and looked over his shoulder at the sixteen statues. "I tell you Jack, I told them idiots that they'd never get to that coal. Whole place is weak as the walls on a doublewide. Their business, god love 'em. Lightning's been touching that stuff off forever. Can't be all that much of the coal left by now. That's why I sold it to 'em. Easy money and a good source of hot-shit amusement for me."

"Been burning ever since I've been around," added

Jack. He looked along Mad Woman Gulch. "Guess I'm glad someone's making money off those bastards. I hate 'em."

"Hate's a powerful word, boy. Careful if I was you on using' that so fuckin' easily. No damn good can come of it," said Elmer.

"I do hate them, Elmer," said Jack and his face grew dark. "Sons of bitches throw their money around and think they can rape the land. Yuppies and coal companies, don't know which is worse. Fuck them all."

"Calm your ass down. No sense in getting' a hard-on this early in the day, least not for a coal company." Elmer laughed and winked at his friend, who smiled and reached for the pint. The old man continued, "Only signs of life I ever saw on that worthless piece-of-shit, burned-out flat were dead ones. Over on the edges of the burning seams I seen bunches of shriveled-up rattlesnakes. Piles of 'em. Must a been drawn to the heat. Fucking reptiles. Don't have a brain in their heads. If they do, can't be no bigger than a piece of buckshot. Those snakes look like big, old used condoms. Ugly sight. Just plain ugly."

"Lovely image there, Elmer."

"Thank you. Always knew you were a man of taste," and the two shared another laugh." And I've seen some kind of dog tracks. Big suckers, too. Maybe five, six inches across. Shit, maybe more. Deep claw marks to 'em. Probably one of Coaker's mastiffs out scavenging those dead snakes. Saw 'em chomping away on an old tractor tire once. Be scared shitless to fall asleep around 'em. Probably chew my legs off or worse if you get my drift," and he thought that was pretty funny. "Keerist, those things are big. Little rain on the paw prints and they wash out to the size of a fucking buffalo wolf. Haven't seen one of those miserable two-hundred pound pricks since I was a boy," he said while killing off the pint. "Coaker's dad trapped it using a dead steer for bait. Must a been three, four feet at the shoulder. Teeth like spikes. Mean looking' piece of dog crap. Damn glad they're gone."

"Sure do get your share of lightning bolts over there, don't you, Elmer?" said Jack. "Haven't had a strike here in years. Last one nailed that old tree behind the pump house and that's been it. Been awhile."

"You're a blessed man. Truly blessed," and the old man leaned towards Jack and winked. "Know what I mean? Don't suppose any of those fires are anything more than accidental do you? Just God's work. My hands are clean, so is my damn conscience for a change," and he turned to the truck and yelled "Cut the shit, dammit. Enough is enough you lame-brained mongrels. Knock it off," and turned back to Jack with another wink. "They think they're getting' to me. No damn way I'll let those weasel-dicked, fleabags get under my skin," and with that he climbed back into the ugly-green truck. "Listen up here a minute. Pay attention, dammit. If I were you, Jack old boy, I'd check into your holdings. Ya know what I'm getting at. Oil and that goddamned coal. Be nice to know what you own and what you don't. And that water of yours may be worth a pretty damn penny to Dark Star, too," and he didn't wink this time. "And remember one more thing, and I don't part with this shit for just anyone. They can come and they can go." He looked straight into Jack's eyes, then fired up the truck, the engine catching with a loud, catarrhal roar and the bunch of them, man and silent dogs, high-tailed it down the road. The Boykins swayed some with the liftoff, but other than that, they didn't move.

He watched them leave, watched the dust settle in the stillness and thought, thought for a long time about what Elmer had said. 'Those fires. Did he set them?

Could he be that crazy or that smart? Mineral rights. Hell I own those. Better check into it though. Old fart's pretty short with his advice so I'd best pay attention. The water? All I've got is that creek, a hot spring and a few stock ponds. What was the old fool trying to tell me? He knows something or is trying to get me worked up for some reason. And what in the hell did he mean by 'they can come and they can go?' Guy's plain crazy. That's all.'

At the same moment Jack was asking himself questions, Elmer was barreling along an open stretch of road at upwards of fifty-miles-per-hour. The gravel and dirt lane ran across a vast, treeless sage flat. 'The boy probably thinks I'm off my rocker, but the kid won't listen to any advice I shoot at 'em straight on. So what if he thinks I'm batty. That's his problem. I ain't no damn fool. No way.'

Five antelope zipped into view, rising fast up out of a brushy draw. They ran alongside the truck for miles keeping Elmer and the dogs company. All of them as wild as the Workman Plateau and its weather.

-TWO-

HOT. UNBEARABLE. NO WIND. *Not so much as a taste of breeze. Only the killing heat reflecting up from the pavement and blasting off the cracked and chipped brick walls that defined the alley, slamming into him, searing his throat. Thirst that was overpowering. Water, cool, clear water was a tormenting dream taking on sensuous dimensions. No clouds in the sky. No blue either. All above was cooked to a glowing white. The blazing sun beat down, sizzling through his body. Sweat drenched him. Soaked his shirt and pants. Tasting of salt, raunchy nicotine and stale whiskey, it ran down his face and poured off his chin and splattered at his feet. The glare of this new, always-the-same day blinded him. Orange, green and yellow circles wavered on the periphery of his vision. All else was in shades of brilliant silver and gold. The stench of melting tar was overpowering. He gagged, then tried to throw up. Thick, grey-brown phlegm was all. His stomach was empty. He hadn't eaten since ... since, hell, he couldn't remember that one either. Something was behind him. He could hear the huge feet of the beast pounding on the cement only yards away, coming closer, could hear the thing panting and growling as it closed in on him. Horror. Fear that drove him mad and made him beg for the strength to run forever. He paused, as if this mattered. No matter how fast he pumped his cramping legs, he remained in the same place. Right*

41

here below the crackling power lines and below the open windows to an empty apartment. Always empty. Same as this alley. No sign of life. No cars. No feral cats stalking rats. No pigeons. No sound. Nothing. And when he looked behind him far down the alley to the empty street, a place out of reach, a distance not measured in feet or miles but instead in bad dreams, there was no nightmarish animal, drooling jaws agape revealing rows of filthy yellow teeth. No hellhound or rabid wolf. Nothing. All there was in this existence for him now was an absolute nothing but his fears, a blankness of such numbing magnitude it had taken on a psychotic aura of purity, of insane absolution. He turned back and then looked far ahead. The street up that way was empty, too. Not even the sound of cars and trucks. But the animal was behind him again. Right behind him. He could feel its damp breath and hear the thing as it sucked the air out of the alley and into its lungs. The creature's nails tore at the pavement, and he looked back to see his death. Nothing. And he ran for the street up ahead of him, ran until his legs gave out and he collapsed and as he fell he could feel the carnivore leaping, anticipated the crunching of bones and ripping of flesh. Could already smell the blood pouring from his wounds. He knew the beast was there behind him and when he turned he could hear its savage roar and smell the rankness of its killing nature, and when he turned back on all of this he could see nothing but the other empty street framed by millions of miles of baking red bricks.' God, is this forever?' and he screamed, a sound that rose from the hell of his soul and the light of this eternal agony blazed through his eyes and this went on forever.

~ ~ ~

They were sitting in an office for Dark Star's

holdings near the very small town of McCoy. Nothing more than a post office-general store-gas station-second-floor-residence and a whitewashed wooden flagpole displaying the country and state flags, both rectangles of cloth ragged around the edges from their constant twenty-four-hour-a-day flapping in the wind. The place was guarded by an old, greying yellow lab, if by guarding was meant lifting his head an inch or two in semi-comatose acknowledgment of the infrequent customer. This was McCoy. This was two days after the loss of the man and the truck over on Yoter's property. The dead man's family in West Virginia had been notified by the operations manager the night of the incident as the company was now referring to the tragedy. The mother broke down and wept. The father took over until he was told that there were no remains and then he fell apart. A friend grabbed the receiver and finished up the gruesome call, barely. He was crying when he hung up. The charred wreckage that had been a pickup truck up until a few days ago was lying in a heap in the gravel lot. All the men present at the meeting could see the mess. They only had to look out one of the wide windows. There were six men sitting around a cigarette-burn scarred maple table. The three survivors, the operations manager, a geologist and a corporate VP flown in last night by company jet from Denver. A FAX machine and a computer quietly hummed along one wall. A coffee urn bubbled away on a stout table next to another wall.

The men discussed damage control in the media. Mainly the operations manager and Bill Foxen, the VP, with occasional nods and brief comments from the others. Because of the somewhat bizarre nature of the death on Yoter's property, the story had gone national with aerial views of the disaster scene flashing across the airwaves. The situation was really no big deal to

Dark Star. They'd weathered much worse than this over the years – deadly cave-ins and explosions back east, ugly evictions of landowners in Utah, photos of the scars left from the strip mine here running in a national magazine then picked up by the major wire services, the usual. They'd ride out this minor glitch in the proceedings until it faded from view, perhaps in a couple of weeks or so. Condolences. A payoff of sorts to the dead man's family. The much larger issue was what to do about the coal the Consortium had paid good money for on Yoter's place.

After a couple of hours of input from the other five, Foxen leaned back and lit a Cuban Flor de Cano cigar with a trio of stick matches. He held the flames from the first two matches just below the end of the cigar, rotating the thick Churchill between his thumb and forefinger slowly in the heat of the invisible upper end of the matches' flames until the tobacco began to smoke slightly. With the third match he put the cigar to his mouth and drew on it slowly. The tip of the Cuban cigar flamed briefly then died down. Foxen sucked in a large mouthful of smoke, savored the rich, spicy taste, then exhaled through pursed lips a thick cloud of blue-grey smoke that partially obscured the VP's face for a few seconds. He held the cigar out in front of him and admired its even brown color and perfect, cylindrical shape. He smoked in silence for nearly twenty minutes as the others fidgeted. Finally he leaned forward while exhaling a huge cloud of mangled smoke.

"This comes down to the basics," he said in a lazy southern Rockies voice. The VP was close to seventy but looked to be in his late-fifties. "Do we go after that coal or don't we? Do we write all this off as an operating loss or do we take the risk and go after that stuff out there?" and he jerked a thumb over his shoulder in the direction of Yoter's place. "My decision is, and I have the authority to make it, my decision is we go after that coal. We do whatever it takes."

The operations manager nodded in agreement. The other four men were stunned. After all that had happened and the more than likely vastly diminished state of the reserves on Yoter's fifty-three sections, they figured that it was a foregone conclusion that Dark Star would back away. They were dead wrong.

"We have the capital right now. We're in good shape," the VP continued. "And we want to send a message not only to the industry, but to the people living out here, that when we buy the rights to something, come hell or high water, we're damn well going to have our way.

"Even if we only pull out a third of what we originally estimated is buried over there, we'll show a decent profit and make a big point," he said with an arrogant grin that was wrapped around the butt of his fat cigar. "This is how we'll proceed, and Pete, I'm counting on you to organize this action and, if necessary, ram-rod it through to its conclusion.

Operations manager Pete Kilduff, a sandy-haired man of medium but wiry build, in his middle forties, nodded. He'd been in difficult spots like this before. Like the one down in Utah, and he loved not only the challenge but the controversy and the energy that swirled around this type of mayhem.

"You got it, Mr. Foxen," Kilduff said in a deep Texas drawl. Kilduff and the VP were long-time friends, but Kilduff always called the man Mr. Foxen in front of other workers. Helped to bring home in a subtle way that Dark Star functioned down through the chain of command, top to bottom, like the military. "My word on it."

"I already knew that Pete." The two shared an inside smile born of playing hardball against all comers over the years. "I want that aquifer beneath Graves' place tapped and those coal fires put out. Start in on the water rights negotiating and slam his ass with the fact that Daddy fucked him out of his mineral rights to pay off gambling debts and his drinking and whoring up in Miles City. While you're doing this, start drilling over in Mad Woman Gulch on Yoter's property. Angle in on that Graves' water from the side. Near as I can figure from these maps it's only a 17-degree pitch..."

"Closer to fifteen, boss," said Kilduff as the other four men watched this whole unbelievable course of action unfold. They'd never been in this ballpark before and were at once frightened and excited. "I've already ordered the crew to ready the rig and bring up the new bits that came in from East Carbon. We should be set to go in a week at the most. We can skirt the burning turf and drive in over the draw just to the south. Sand wash on top but firm underneath. She'll hold our rigs. A little aggregate and some grading is all it'll take."

"Good man," said the VP as he worked on the cigar and doodled on a note pad. Just lines and vector arrows pointing in all directions drawn in blue ballpoint. "And dig up anything you can on that Jack Graves clown and that woman. What's her name?" He shuffled through a thick file before finding what he was looking for. "Krietner. Natalie Krietner. Good-looking woman. Too good looking for that fool. Must be something kinky going on with them. Find out what it is. Photos if you can. Any questions?"

"Just one," said Kilduff. "What's the budget on this one?"

"Sky's the limit," said the VP. "You've got my authorization with the boys in Denver." The VP stood up. "Any other questions?" There were none. "Good. I've got an appointment for dinner in an hour." With a woman young enough to be my daughter, he thought.

"Pete, call me in the morning before I head back to Denver."

Foxen mashed out his cigar in a coffee cup and strode out the door. The meeting was over.

~ ~ ~

He was in bed with two of them. Legs, arms, breasts, sweaty hair, lingerie, the whole works. Cow town whores. Fifty bucks apiece all night. Whiskey, gin bottles and glasses filled with the booze were scattered about the room. Ashtrays filled with jammed out cigarette butts. He'd come up from his ranch on the Workman two nights ago and had been gambling, drinking and fucking ever since. For a change he hadn't lost a lot of money at cards. He had card sense, when he was reasonably sober, which wasn't most of the time up here. Normally on these three-day binges he would leave town a couple of grand lighter from the poker, and there was the liquor and women. Not this time. He finished up last night a few hundred ahead. He'd been drunk when he engaged the ladies and the three of them had been at it all night. All sorts of convoluted positions and combinations and as this new day approached, the dawn light starting to show as a soft grey through the room's lone window, he was played out. He got up and drained a glass of last night's bourbon sitting on the dresser and then one filled with stale gin. He fought to keep the liquor down as it burned and boiled in his stomach. He told the two women to go back to sleep and left a pair of fifties on the bedside table for the ladies, dressed, walked out the door, quietly closing it behind, down the dingy hall and out onto the street to get some coffee and breakfast at a cafe around the corner.

The waitress brought coffee without asking and he ordered eggs easy over, hash browns, sausage, toast and juice. 'Takes stamina to keep this up,' he thought and laughed quietly. Not a happy sound. He stirred a heaping spoonful of sugar in the coffee and drained the cup in one take. The waitress had it refilled before he could look up to signal her that he needed more. Then she was gone. She'd seen his kind before. Men living out their private hells and warring with their demons. She left him alone.

Jack Graves Sr. liked to think of himself as a good man, an honest one, but like most men who'd lived some, he knew better. Getting through the day-to-day involved making choices and doing things he was, at best, uncomfortable with. His wasn't a glamorous existence. Cattle and lots of hard work, month after month in dry, harsh, relentless country. Didn't make much money at it, either. Life with his wife was at best a series of accommodations, acquiescence and subtle humiliations. They hadn't had sex together in years, since shortly after their son, Jack Jr., was born. Before this she had been extremely aggressive and adventuresome, showing him things about sex he had never even thought of. And Kate dressed to please him. Wore her hair long the way he liked. Silky slips and panties. Garter belts and stockings. She kept him in a constant state of arousal. But since the birth of their son she had changed, cutting her hair short, wearing nothing but jeans and loose-fitting flannel shirts, and, worst of all, hideous flannel nightgowns to bed. He felt like he was sleeping with his mother. So, as far as their love life went, there was none. At first she'd stalled him saying things like 'This will pass in a few months as soon as I recover from being pregnant' or 'You're always brooding and yelling. I'm too angry to sleep with you' or, and this was his favorite, 'I should never have married you in the first place. All I wanted out of this was a son and now I have that. And, you call this a life,' Then she'd look around their modest home and

48

out the window at the lonesome land that rolled away for miles. He'd tried to reason with her, but Kate never wavered from this statement and often added 'I never loved you to begin with. Never.' She had all the answers and was waiting with a logical roadblock at every turn, or if he somehow managed to make a point, put a dent in her labyrinthine logic, she would shut him out of her life with one withering look, go for days without speaking to him and sleep in the spare room. Eventually she'd worn him down and he gave up on satisfying his physical desires and his need to be close to her in that way. He turned, as most men of faithful intentions do under these circumstances, to masturbation, but this wore thin after a couple of years. Unfulfilling to the point of boredom, even to depression. But this wasn't enough for her. She needed to further control and humiliate him. She pointedly stared at muscular, younger men when she and Jack went to town. And she would touch him suggestively in all the right places until he became excited, then she would back off and start talking about something inane like how the tomato plants were doing or the weather. She'd been doing this for years and when he could no longer stand it, he'd try and force himself on her, but Kate would yell and say she wasn't interested in him and never would be, and she'd 'be damned' if she'd sleep with a no-good whiskey drunk. And when she really began to hammer him over drinking whiskey after he'd completed a day's work or occasionally playing cards with his friends, he'd finally had enough.

Ten years ago on a trip to Mikes City, a cow town with modest expectations and a number of decent bars, while picking up some parts for his tractor along with a new hot water heater, he made a decision. The bearings for the tractor didn't come into the parts store until after five and the water heater wouldn't arrive at the appliance place until the next morning. He'd called his wife, explained the situation, said he'd get a room in town and be back by mid-afternoon at the latest and she sighed like he was the one responsible for the delays and hung up. Pissed off, he went to the nearest bar and poured down shots of whiskey which he chased with schooners of Grain Belt beer. After eating a chicken-fried steak and a pile of mashed potatoes smothered with gravy and fried onions at the bar, he adjourned to the back room and its non-stop poker game. Ranchers in for the day, slickers, drifters with a few bucks in their pockets, local businessmen, there was always a game in the smoky, windowless back room. Sometimes for decent stakes. He played until past midnight and lost a little money. Forty dollars. Then he pushed away from the table, bought a bottle of whiskey from over the bar and walked out onto the dimly lit street and the drizzle. His room in an old, derelict hotel was only a block away.

Before he'd gone twenty paces one of Miles City's numerous hookers approached him and asked if he needed someone to share his bottle with. He'd never been unfaithful to his wife. Never even considered it, but without hesitation, without asking the cost, he said "Sure. Why the hell not," and the two went off to his room with the lady draped around him. In the dingy room – single bed, grey linen, washstand, night table, no lamp, bare light bulb overhead – the two smoked cigarettes and worked on the bottle. He poured out his miseries concerning his marriage. She was a good whore. She listened and touched his knee and then his thigh during particularly traumatic junctures in his narrative. Then she got up and took off her clothes and stood before him in the sheerest of white panties and bra. He instantly forgot about his problems and his excitement was clearly visible when the whore undid his zipper. In what seemed an instant to him, they were in bed and she had him inside her. After years without sex with a woman, the sensation of her rocking up and down while she straddled him, the warm, moistness, was beyond memory, beyond anything he'd ever experienced. It had been that long. He squeezed her firm breasts in his hands pinching her erect nipples and he arched up to get into her still further. When he came, he groaned "Oh, Jesus!" and sank back into the bed. The whore wasted little time. She climbed off him, cleaned herself at the washstand, dressed, took a twenty from his wallet, bent over and kissed him on the forehead, and left the room. He was up for hours reliving the all-too-short experience, finally falling asleep near 4 A.M. A few hours later he awoke resolved to make this a regular part of his life. He'd done without the basic pleasures for far too long. The hell with his wife and her frigidity. He was a man. He was alive, goddamnit, and he smiled at this newfound vehemence and determination. He hopped in the pickup, picked up the tractor parts and the water heater, then drove home down along the badlands that pushed up to the Workman River. He sipped whiskey and beer on the way home, driving at a leisurely 40 miles-per-hour on the oiled-dirt road. He was enjoying himself. His new, almost euphoric mood did not go unnoticed by Kate, and women being women she pretty well figured out what had happened up in Miles City. She clamped down and made the past years of privation and torment look like a vacation. She turned his life into hell in so many carefully thought out, subtle ways, Jack thought he was going to kill her. She knew his every move and his every thought and she played these to her own wicked perfection. Everything in their relationship was the same only always shifting slightly to either keep him off-balance or angry or hurt. Objects around the house were slightly moved. His eggs were just barely undercooked. His jeans were still neatly folded in his dresser, but just barely damp. She made seemingly innocuous comments about how his hair looked or the state of his boots. And she would move his whiskey from cupboard to cupboard with no discernible pattern or rhythm. He'd spend long minutes looking for it until she would walk over to a certain shelf and grab the booze with an angry I can't believe-you-forgot-where-the-damn-stuff-was flourish. He'd snatch the bottle from her, stomp out onto the front porch, collapse into a wicker chair and drink straight from the bottle, the bourbon tasting sharp and fiery in his mouth. And so on. He was being driven crazy and they both knew it, knew that she was enjoying the hell out of herself putting him through this never-ending misery. He was desperate. He needed to get back to the planned drunkenness, the cards and, most of all, the whores in Miles City, but times were tough and he was short on cash for such doings.

As is so often the case, fortunately or unfortunately, depending on one's perspective, the solution to this difficulty walked right up to him while he was in Drew running errands. He'd stopped at The Mint for a couple of quick ones and his life changed.

He knocked back his second shot of bar whiskey and took a sip of beer, lit a Pall Mall, then leaned his elbows on the scarred wooden bar and rested his unshaved chin on his fists. A couple of stools down a man in crisp jeans, checked shirt with pearl-inlaid buttons, and new straw hat pushed back on his head, was talking to the bartender in a medium-volumed voice that had a suggestion of Texas in it, but not much of one. He was tanned and looked fit, hard and lean, probably in his late twenties.

Tell ya the truth, Dutch," said the guy. "I miss the

hustle and the A-Rabs over there in the Middle East. Crazy bastards drink their own piss to purify their bodies and the way they treat their women. If we tried that here, we'd be castrated. But I don't miss all the heat and sand. Stuff got into everything. My eyes were always red and burning and my skin was rubbed raw before it turned rough like cheap leather. Mark my words," he said in a soft drawl. "Someday them desert savages are going to be worth more money than anyone ever thought existed. It's that goddamned oil lying beneath all that sand. Those camel drivers are going to be filthy rich," and he sipped from his drink.

"And when you look at it, this buying up the mineral rights around here is tedious, hell, make that down-right boring, at times, but Northern High Plains is a good company to work for. Medical, decent pay and incentives and plenty of time to myself. Just got the rights over on Vallie Eave's place up along Hayne's Coulee sewed up yesterday. Lots of coal on that land. Can see some of it along the edges of the land where it breaks off. One hundred sections give or take for thirty an acre comes to close to two million and I make one-point-five percent on that or thirty thousand. Mind you, that's in addition to my salary. Three or four of those a year and I'm doing okay. More than okay," and the man flashed a big grin that let Dutch know this was someone who was sure he had the world by the balls.

Graves leaned a bit the man's way, sipped his beer and pointed to his shot glass and to the man's glass. Dutch filled them both and took a couple of bucks from the pile in front of Graves, who leaned over and introduced himself and asked what the deal was with the coal.

"Glad to meet ya, Jack," and the man slid off his stool and walked over and shook hands with a firm grip. "Name's Bill Foxen. Work for Northern High

Plains Coal out of Gillette. I've been buying the mineral rights from ranchers around here. Helping you folks out with a load of cash they didn't expect to have. Mainly coal we're interested in. Nothing as big as what Dark Star is starting up by McCoy. We just want to get a foothold in this country. Sort of looking' off in the future, you might say. Probably won't even consider working any of it 'til well into the next century if even then. Hell, we make money on taxes just by spending money," and Bill drained his drink and nodded for a round for each of them and added "Pour a stiff one for yourself, Dutch," and turned back to Jack Sr.. "Beats me all to hell how a company can make dough by spending it, but that's the way she shakes out, at least so they tell me.'

The answer to Graves' cash woes was right here if this man was interested. Over seven thousand acres at thirty per was more than two-hundred thousand. Enough to pay off the last loan on his land and home, and more than enough to go up to Miles City or, what the hell, even as far west as Butte, whenever he wanted. Man can raise all sorts of Cain in that town.

He and Bill discussed the eleven sections, where it was located and if he had clear title to the land. Bill told him he'd meet Graves out by the road that dropped down into Mad Woman Gulch at seven tomorrow morning. Kate was up in Great Falls visiting one of her friends for the next week and maybe he could sneak this deal through without her knowing.

They had a few more drinks and he let Bill in on a portion of his woes and the need to do the deal on the sly. Bill said "No problem" as long as the land was in Jack's name and he said he'd bring the papers, including the ones showing that he needed to pay off around thirty thousand to free-up everything. The man from Northern High Plains was out to buy the rights to ranchers' coal, whatever it took. Going behind the back of this guy's wife was part of doing business, closing the deal. Bill said he had access to an attorney on a retainer for Northern High Plains that could draw up the agreement in such a way it would take a sharp lawyer to figure out what had happened, that Jack had sold his mineral rights to someone else. Bill said he understood about women and how they wanted to run everything and poke their noses into "business that concerns only men." He'd take care of everything. The payment, if things panned out would be "No problem," according to Bill. Eleven sections, while "A fair piece of land," in Bill's words, wouldn't "hardly put a dent in the company's acquisition fund." And Foxen was as good as his word. The coal on Graves' land was well below the surface, but the company figured in time the country's need for energy would drive the price of the stuff up to the point where digging down hundreds of feet would still turn a profit. According to current surveys the seams on Jacks' land ran from twenty-three to thirty feet thick. He let Jack think that he'd driven a hard bargain, that he was a shrewd businessman-rancher, finally settling on thirty-three bucks an acre after initially offering twenty-eight. Foxen was prepared to go to forty and he earned another little bonus for coming in under this figure. All told, figuring in taxes and legal fees, Graves walked away with close to two hundred thousand.

When Kate returned he told her he'd decided to pay off the bank by closing his savings account which had about thirty-seven thousand in it. Before she could make a scene he showed her the clear titles to their property and home in both their names, and a term life-insurance policy he took out on himself for half-a-million with her as the sole beneficiary paid up for ten years. He also gave her a thousand in cash that was left over saying "I just wanted you to feel secure in case anything happened to me," and she actually smiled a real smile and gave him a genuine hug. She liked material things a lot. Not as much as she loved her son, but a lot. During this rare show of affection Jack was thinking 'Fuck you Kate. I've got enough money to do whatever I damn please now," and he smiled while hugging her.

Within a month the deal was done. Graves sat in his truck parked on the street outside the Northern High Plains' office in Drew reading over all the legal documents, especially the title agreement and the language describing the fact that Northern High Plains Coal owned the mineral rights. His eyes crossed and his brain got fuzzy just trying to put the words together as he read the elaborate legal jargon. 'No way in hell could Kate figure out this lawyer bullshit.'

'The hell with her,' he thought. 'She loves the damn kid more than me. Hell she only puts up with me because I have the strength to take her crap. I'm nothing but a fucking punching bag to her. Fuck you Kate. I hate you. Can't believe I ever loved you.' He didn't hate his son. That would come later. For now he resented the kid and was jealous of all the affection his mother showered on Jack Jr. He promised himself he'd never let his son know how he really felt about either him or his mother. No good purpose served by that went his reasoning. 'What a sick damn life I'm stuck in' and he took a deep swig from a pint of whiskey, then cleared his throat and spit out the truck's window. He fired up the aging pickup, drove out of town and turned onto the long road that climbed on top of Workman Plateau and led to the ranch. "Fuck 'em all," he said out loud.

~ ~ ~

From the top of Chambers Point Jack Jr. could see

for nearly seventy miles in any direction. The unspoiled bluff country of southeastern Montana stretched from horizon to horizon, thousands of square miles of ragged coulees, Ponderosa pine forest, sagebrush and native grasslands. Infinite variations on shades of red, pink, orange, yellow, grey, green, blue. This was one of the least-known parts of a little-known land. To reach where he was standing took two hours of lurching and crawling his old truck over rocky two-tracks that eventually faded away to nothing. Then a few more dusty, hot hours scrambling and crawling up steep cuts littered with broken rock. To reach the top of the place you paid with sweat, blood from skinned knuckles, palms and knees, burning lungs and cramping leg muscles as you clawed and pushed through the rubble to gain a thousand feet in elevation. The surrounding sea of hills and crumbling sandstone cliffs stood out in stark relief against a cloudless dome of sky. In extremely dry country this wasted piece of it was a desert. The place was without water. Storms would build in the west, enormous clouds billowing thousands of feet above black shrieking bases of roiling rain and hail. Bolts of lightning, cloud and earth fought in electric violence. Rain fell in torrents as the heavy weather swept over the plains. Then the massive clouds would shrivel up and vanish like smoke in the wind before they deposited so much as a drop of rain around Chambers Point; or the rain would fall only to evaporate back into the sky, never reaching this forsaken rock and dirt. Even cactus was in short supply here, mostly pods of prickly pear that were shrunken, desiccated. Clumps of sere Blue bunch wheatgrass clung to tan-colored soil baked as hard as concrete. Dry washes were worn smooth by the wind. There were no signs of fresh cutting from the rushing runoff of infrequent spring downpours common to the rest of the Workman Plateau. For some reason this outcrop repelled the rain. Through some force the rocky point pushed it away. So, there wasn't any water here, except for a tiny spring near the summit of the point. A moist anomaly that somehow, by a curious construction in the layered rock, was forced upward in a meandering path until the water seeped out far above the plateau on this blasted point of nowhere. A miracle of sorts that vanished within a few yards of its source. A meager trickle of warm liquid that spread its life out in a small, irregular circle of olive-green moss and diminutive specimens of Threadleaf Phacelia, the plants' delicate pink flowers an incongruous sight shining in the spring sunlight high up here in the midst of this pile of barren desolation and parched chaos. Even rattlesnakes were rare in the Chambers formation. Jack had spotted perhaps a half dozen in the thirty years he'd been struggling into this pocket of isolation where he'd never encountered another soul, all the snakes not far from the water, sunning themselves on narrow ledges and not even bothering to rattle at his passing.

For some reason the biggest turkeys he'd ever seen hid out in this trackless mayhem. Unexplainable as was so much of what happened on the plateau below. Here were ridges and belts of rock that looked like they had been heaved up and then slammed around by an enormous and fearsome being trapped in an uncontrollable rage. Epochs of these striations sliced through one another without order. Precambrian sedimentary rock shoved between Tertiary gravels in diagonal thrusts. Mesozoic shale, limestone and sandstone ran brightly within this in horizontal bands of ochre, tan and grey. Proterozoic, Pliocene, Triassic, all mixed together in a scene of such gigantic disorder, it was past comprehension. Why the turkeys picked this place was beyond Jack. He'd killed a thirty-two-pounder when he was in his teens, back when he'd first found this area by accident one day while roaming these isolated roads on his way back from the Bucking Horse Sale in Miles City. He was hooked as soon as he stepped out of the truck and looked up at Chambers Point. Again, he couldn't explain the fascination any more than he could his little stream and even smaller brown trout. Some places called to him powerfully and he always answered, was unable to resist the force of the land when it spoke to him. Two years ago he killed an even larger bird. There was little mast for the turkeys to feed on save for the bunchgrass. No Ponderosa pine cones. No grain from ranchers' fields. Nothing. A few crickets and near-dead grasshoppers. And the only water was this little spring. Yet, the large birds came to this microscopic oasis every day at sunset during late-April. Jack wasn't into trophies, but fighting his way up here, hiding behind a pile of shattered sandstone downwind of the spring and head-shooting one of these enormous turkeys was the flip-side to the thrill he got fishing for his little brown trout back home.

He'd packed a bedroll, a little food – nuts, dried fruit, jerky, a bottle of whiskey, water, some bandages and codeine-based painkillers in case he hurt himself. Nothing else, save for his rifle, pocketknife and some matches. He liked to be out in this empty country with as little as possible and what he brought was always enough. Hunched down against the rocks out of the wind at night sipping the whiskey and maybe even enjoying the sharp flickering of the smallest of twig fires, the wood scrounged on his way up, he felt free, unburdened from all of the madness and anxiety down below. He was part of all this emptiness and he never felt more alive. Nothing compared to the time he spent on top of Chambers Point.

"Lived here all my life," he said to the wind. The sun was edging down towards the western horizon, going from blaze yellow to intense orange as it declined in the sky. "One life too many it seems. Completely fuckin' nuts, that's all there is to it," and he took a sip of water and ducked back down behind the rocks.

Earlier in the day he'd driven into town and dropped off title papers, sale agreements and anything else related to his ownership of the ranch for his attorney to examine. Elmer's words of the other day had registered. The lawyer's secretary took them with an outstretched hand and a sincere smile saying that Jim would look them over and give him a call next week. Jack said that was fine, drove home, loaded the gear and now he was here. Something in Elmer's words had triggered a warning within him and the state of affairs concerning the mineral rights bothered him. Coming to Chambers Point was a way of clearing his mind and catching his breath. He looked out over the country to the north. At night he could see the lights of Miles City, a real cow town dying an ugly death at the hands of developers and yuppies. They had latched onto the town after a barrage of articles about the annual May bucking horse sale and all the "real west" goings on. Now the south side of town was strip developed, littered with a K-Mart, Wal-Mart, McDonalds, Mini-Mart – the whole nine yards of junk and bargain-priced greed that eventually revealed its astronomical true price. And the streets and parking lots were filled with SUVs, BMWs, Hummers and the like driven by Californians and East Coasters who'd accumulated tons of money doing nothing but fucking each other over in the stock market and in similar valueless venues. Twelve-thousand-square -foot homes looking for all the world like participants in a lunatic architectural big-dick contest now clung to the hillsides above the Yellowstone River and out on the grassy floodplains. Bistros and coffee kiosks abounded. 'The real west my ass,' Jack thought as he looked up Miles City way and thought about what was going on there. How soon would the malignancy reach the old bars and stores on Main Street? When would the ranch hands and old-timers be forced out of their watering holes? 'Fucking yuppies trash everything they touch. Shit all over a place and on those of us who call it home. God help the fuckers if I ever find out I have cancer,' and he took a small sip of water. 'Thank God they can't see what this country really is. With my luck the useless shits will latch onto rock hounding the way they strangled fly-fishing. Dickheads will haul the country away in their four-wheel-drive Cadillacs and Range Rovers one bag of rocks at a time,' and he spit in the direction of town. 'Worthless shits. They produce nothing that matters and ruin what means something to the rest of us.' He laughed at his internal tirade and concentrated on calming down. Turkeys were spooky as hell, had radar for the rage he was broadcasting. Minutes passed and he dropped into the timeless rhythm of the mangled hills.

He turned slowly and peered through a crack in the rocks. 'Jesus Christ!' he said to himself. 'Never heard it coming. Biggest damn bird I've ever seen,' and he looked once more. 'Thirty-five pounds. Maybe larger. Beard must be a foot if it's an inch. Damn!'

He took five minutes soundlessly moving the .22 into position. He lined the barrel's bead on the turkey's head, on its unblinking eye. He curled his finger around the trigger and began to gently squeeze. Then he stopped and stared as the bird dipped its big head up and down as it pecked at something in the spongy moss. He felt like he was being watched. The hairs on his neck were standing up. He carefully looked behind him. Nothing. No one. Jack started to pull on the trigger once more, but again he stopped. The feeling of being watched grew stronger and he turned once again. Still nothing. 'Damn strange. Weird.' And he watched the bird over the top of the bead on the .22, the turkey unaware of his presence.

'Can't kill this one. Maybe the only bird this size in Montana, hell the whole damn West,' and he stood up. If turkeys could look stunned, this one did. Standing erect, at least four feet tall, it looked right at Jack then let loose with a series of wild gobbles as it fled, feathers tucked tight to its thick body, downhill and out of sight.

"I could have killed that bird, easy," he said. "Couldn't bring myself to do it. Never see anything like that again in my life." He walked over to the spring and looked at the tracks the Tom had left in the moist, sandy soil and in the moss. Three-pronged prints almost as big as his hand etched in the soil and pressed down in the moss, that was rapidly regaining its original form. Droppings as thick as delicious-sized cigars. "More than thirty-five pounds. God what a bird."

He stood there on top of Chambers Point for a long time. The sensation of someone watching him passed. He thought about this before saying "Completely nuts. That's all there is to it."

Jack looked out over the land until well after the sun went down and the eternal, countless stars came out.

~ ~ ~

At the same time Jack was drawing down on the turkey, several miles northwest of Chambers Point a lone wolf loped along a game trail following the fresh tracks and droppings of several mule deer who had passed this way not long before. The well-traveled path was worn several inches into the soil and paralleled

Philly Joe coulee. This particular solitary wolf dwarfed the gray wolves that ran in the beleaguered Magic, Wigwam and Camas packs in Glacier Park country or those hapless canine souls who had been reintroduced or, more accurately, kidnapped from their territories somewhere else in the northwest, and dumped into Yellowstone Park. This wolf picked off a scent riding the cooling southeast wind. The animal stopped and sniffed. The clear odor of man coming down to it from a rocky point outlined sharply against the sky sent a shiver along its deep tan, grey and white body. It raised its enormous muzzle into the air for a better taste. The wolf was familiar with the scent, had encountered it for years. In the past, at the first whiff, the merest suggestion of contact with humans, the animal had turned tail and vanished into obscure niches of the obscure country. But not this time. Something in the way this man smelled, and the wolf was quite capable of telling a man from a woman, some slight coloring around the edges of his scent, stopped the animal in its tracks and caused it to stare for a long time in the direction the wind was coming from. There were the odors that signaled predator and death but there was something more, something wild like the wolf itself, perhaps another animal of the wild with no rules to live by except those of freedom and survival. It turned to drift down into the coulee out of harm's way, looking for one last time up at Chambers Point. And then the two-hundred-plus pound beast swiftly and silently vanished.

~ ~ ~

Jack and Natalie were fixing some fence down in the bottom of Mad Woman Gulch. The soil was sandy clay. Several of Jack's peripatetic Angus had pushed against the sagging barbed wire strands and knocked down some rotted wooden posts in the process. Cattle and the weather were always doing a number on his fence lines. Repairing them was a never-ending chore. The cows had wandered the length of the gulch and up onto the bench above where they were inexorably heading towards the burning coal seams. A massive barbecue in the offing. Elmer had spotted the animals while scanning the land through his high-powered telescope, something he did for hours every day when he wasn't highballing it on the back roads with the Boykins, who were still silent according to Elmer. "Not so much as a yip out of 'em, but I'm hanging' in there. They'll break soon, I damn well hope to tell ya," he told Jack over the phone along with the information on his wandering cattle. Jack was having coffee with Natalie at the time. The two of them walked a mile or so, spotted the Angus and ran them back home, scaring the dumb beasts by yelling and waving their arms. The cattle along with a couple of dozen of their less adventuresome compatriots were now standing in the filthy muck and moss that bordered a small stock pond that formed from the meager output of a small off-and-on spring. By July the thing would be nothing more than a small bit of thick, algae-choked soup and cracked mud. A home to millions of flies and a powerful stink.

Jack worked the post hole digger, slammed the blades into the hard ground that lay a couple of feet beneath the clay, twisted the tool around and back-and-forth with his legs, arms and shoulders and then squeezed the thing closed so he could extract a cupful of soil. Hard work beneath the sun, but there were only seven old holes to re-dig. Natalie placed the metal stakes by each hole before dropping them in and kicking rock and dirt around them. Then she used a solid steel breaker bar to tamp down the ground, and repeated the process until each stake was standing upright and rock solid. From time to time Jack would look up from his work, wipe his sweaty forehead on his shirt sleeve, then yell an assortment of obscenities at the Angus as they stared back at him with dumb, dark eyes, viscous drool hanging from their mouths in long strings. Sometimes his tirades would scare the creatures to the extent that they would erupt in explosive outbursts of green-brown, watery shit that splattered on the ground and into the water. At moments like this he'd think 'It's enough to make you give up beef,' then he'd return to slamming the tool into the ground, the sharp metal blades clanging off chunks of rock.

In a couple of hours all of the stakes were set. The two of them used a come-along to winch the four strands of rusting wire tight before attaching it to the posts with wire clips that they twisted with pliers. Finished, they walked over to a large Ponderosa and dropped down in the shade onto a soft, crunching carpet of needles. He pulled a pair of warm beers from the tool kit, popped the tops in a cascade of foam and handed one to her. They each drained off half and looked at the ochre-lime colored cutbank across the gulch. The night before last a heavy thunderstorm had dumped at least an inch of rain amidst a hail of lightning, thunder and tornadic blowings. Common weather on the Workman. A lightning bolt had fried one of Elmer's cows and a gust of wind had crumpled a small chicken coop, incensed and terrified hens clucking all over the place. One of the roosters, quartered in a nearby pen was now up on the peak of the barn roof squawking away. Elmer told Jack he was thinking about "Bringing the damned bird down with my 30.06," but he wasn't sure just yet. Power lines were also down along the roads. Quite a blast. Tons of soil lay in piles and chunks at the bottom of the draw, washed and broken away from the deluge.

The rain had scrubbed the air clean of wind-driven dust. Sunlight sparkled off reflective mineral deposits in the earth glittering like diamonds. Quartz and mica. Moving his head to look up towards Elmer's land, something flashed white. Jack stared hard at the spot and located what looked like an exposed portion of a large skull stuck in the bank about a dozen feet below the surface. A large dark hole, perhaps an eye socket, stared at him. He walked over to the bank, clambered up so that he was eye to eye with the skull. Above him snakes sunning themselves rattled and hissed in the grass growing at the edge of the bank. Steadying himself, he began digging in the loosely packed soil around the bones.

"Nat. I think it's an old buffalo skull," he yelled. "Come over and look." Jack pulled the loose soil from the thing, grasped it with both hands by the jaws and yanked. The ground at his feet and that holding the skull gave way easily and he went flying away from the shelf and down to the bottom of Mad Woman. Chunks and buckets-worth of dirt piled on top of him. The bison skull cracked him on the head as he crash-landed, knocking him senseless. In an instant Natalie was kneeling over him frantically digging and pushing dirt and rock away. Blood was streaming from a large cut in his forehead, the gash being forced ever wider by the rapidly rising knot growing above his right eye. He groaned and rolled over the skull, ripping his shirt on one of the bison's horns. He slowly rose to a sitting position, eyes glazed, head lolling on slumped shoulders.

"Shit that hurt," as blood ran into his eye, down his cheek and onto his jeans. She took her shirt off and ripped it in strips that she then wrapped around his head and tied off in square knots.

"Are you okay, babe? God, you look awful."

He wiped his eyes and his head began clearing. What he saw was unexpected at best, even for Workman country. A huge, probably ancient, buffalo skull at his feet, blood all over his clothes, the bank still crumbling in miniature avalanches of soil and pebbles, and a gorgeous woman leaning over him naked from the waist up, her firm, white breasts holding forth right in front of his face. Reacting instinctively, he reached forward with one gloved hand, grasped the left one and leaned forward to suck its erect nipple.

"Ouch, you damned freak," and she slapped and pushed his head and hand away in one smooth, hard motion. "Jesus! Is that all you men think about. Hell! I thought you might have a concussion or be bleeding to death, but hell no. The first thing you think about is sucking my tits." She looked at him with angry eyes that eventually gave way to the beginnings of a smile and laughter. "You are a freak, buddy. God only knows what you really have on your mind when it comes to sex." She looked away, up to where the skull came from and said softly to herself, out of his hearing, "I guess that's what excites me about you. Not having a clue about what you want from me."

She turned back and commanded, "Take off your shirt and the T-shirt, too."

He did as he was told and started in on the belt and zipper of his pants hoping for the best.

"Not those you moron and sure as hell not here in the dirt with you all bloody," she said scornfully. "Men. You're hopeless. I need the T-shirt for me. Can't be bouncing around out here in the open. That crazy Elmer could be anywhere."

Jack shrugged, zipped his fly and put on his bloodied flannel shirt. Natalie pulled on his sweaty T-shirt. They both stood up and gathered their bearings, shaking the dirt from them, but this was really pointless. Blood, sweat and dirt turned mud, and dust covered them. They looked like hard-rock miners after a day's mean labor. A severe headache was making an appearance behind the knot on his head. Waves of sharp pain were shooting out his eyes. The cut hurt so bad it felt like it was itching and tearing a wide gash across his face at the same time. Natalie retrieved the beers and handed them to Jack. He downed both of them, hot liquid running out the sides of his mouth and down his chin. A coyote barked not far from them, perhaps a few hundred yards down the gulch. 'Damn things are telepathic,' he thought. 'Every time I do anything with her, even think of doing it, one of those damn dogs starts howling away. Crazy animals are so plugged into this place, I can't even open a can of beer without them knowing about it. Middle of nowhere and no privacy at all.'

"What woman in her right mind could resist you," Natalie said as she tried to wipe some dirt and gore from his face. "You're as weird as they come. Grab my boobs after a bloody cave-in. Scare the shit out of your cows. Worship your little brown trout. What else, Jack? What other twisted little things do you have running around in that head? Me playing the man and you the woman? I sure as hell wouldn't put it past you," and she wasn't smiling. Wasn't looking mad either. More like curious, like where do you want to take me?

He looked back and pushed down thoughts that were trying to turn themselves into words, pushed them back out of view and only said "Shit, Nat," before stooping down to the skull and brushing the dirt off of it. With an effort he lifted the mass of soiled bone and shook still more dirt from it. Sand, clay and rock pouring out of eye sockets, the mouth and the neck opening. He held it in the light. Nearly intact. All of the skull structure most of the worn teeth and both horns, large ones that were barely damaged after all these years, centuries. He looked down the rows of teeth towards the back. Embedded in some dried mud was a piece of chipped, black stone. He set the skull down and dug at the object with his fingers. Finally he extracted the six-inch piece. Black and shiny like obsidian and formed into a point, a spear point. He could see the scalloped chisel marks, and when he looked again at the back of the bison skull he noticed a shattered edge along the bone.

"Probably made by the hunters," he said as he held out the spear point to show her and pointed at the damaged bone. "Before horses were introduced, they used to herd the buffalo to cliffs, even small ones like that," and now he aimed a finger at the tall cutbank, "and run them over the edge, then finish them off with spears and large rocks, anything handy. Beat them to death. Must have been something to see." He looked at the skull a long time. "As deep as this buffalo was buried in the ground ... hell, it may be a thousand years old or more, times before the Cheyenne or Crow were out here. Maybe Yantonai Sioux, but who knows for sure when any of them reached this country."

"Give me a hand with this. We'll lug it back and clean it up. I want to hang it over the fireplace. My old man would have loved it. Just his kinda thing." They each took turns carrying it up Jack's side of Mad Woman Gulch, the other lugging the fencing tools. "Starting to really feel like shit, girl. Let's keep pushing."

"You look bad, babe. I'll need to put some stitches in that cut for you."

"Oh shit," and off they went. On the way back she noticed huge dog prints running down the slope they were climbing. She pointed them out to Jack.

"Probably from Coaker's mastiffs running deer. Goddamn those dogs. Elmer's seen them, too. Said the rain makes the tracks look larger than they really are, which already is big." The two continued on, sweating, swearing and trudging back to Jack's place.

On top of a sandstone cliff some miles away the huge wolf picked up the man's scent once again. There was no fear at the taste of human in its nostrils. Only recognition. The animal had worked its way south from Chamber's Point as it had done sporadically for some time. Now the wolf was down here following the faint traces of the man's smell. No reason for this behavior surfaced in the wolf's head. Not questions of why am I doing this or should I be doing this? It was reacting naturally from external stimulus and internal fires, drives. A wild animal roaming the countryside. The wolf lifted its head and screamed an ungodly howl, a sound not heard on the Workman for a very long time. Not for more than eighty years and never with this intensity. The cry died on the wind before ever reaching Jack and Natalie as they worked their way through the pines.

~ ~ ~

Warm, mineral-rich water bubbled up through cracks in the rock making the hot tub-sized pool in the smooth stone appear effervescent. The water poured over a narrow gap in the stone and flowed down into a slim crease in the land, the water cascading down a series of limestone steps until it reached Mad Woman Gulch where it disappeared into the porous soil. The hot springs formed at the head of the draw at a place where cracks and fissures allowed the water to push through to the surface. This country was dotted with such warm outbursts of liquid. Jack and Natalie lounged naked in the warmth and sucked in the moist air that tasted of sulfur mixed with the sweet perfume of the native grasses, sage and wildflowers. Hundreds of striped chorus frogs croaked all around them. Night owls boomed not far away and a lone robin babbled from a tall Ponderosa below them. From their positions in the pool they could see out over the tops of the pines growing below in the ravine, could see for miles and miles across the rolling, green expanse of the plateau with its multi-colored, Ponderosa cloaked bluffs and hills. Natalie had suggested that a long hot soak might ease some of Jack's pain, so the pair had packed a couple of bottles of Merlot and some St. Louis Rey double corona cigars. They walked through the trees behind his place and the quarter-mile through the new, thick grass that was heavy with cool evening dew. Shedding their clothes they slipped into the 109-degree water and sighed as one. Natalie opened one of the bottles of wine, the cork giving way with a small "pop." She bit off the ends of two cigars off, lit them and handed one to Jack. They sat back and drank in the night sky.

The usual countless stars and planets and galaxies were out, but a growing instrument-dash green glow in the north was beginning to overpower the stars. The luminous haze rose above the horizon and boiled like storm clouds. Suddenly narrow streams of intense green shot far into the night sky and sailed over their heads. Next curtains of the diaphanous light shimmered across the entire northern horizon. Streaks of brighter green raced through these with an intensity that cast soft green-black shadows over the grass and sage. Their faces fluoresced in the heavenly radiance. The Northern Lights. Not the blues, whites and reds of the Yukon, but rather the subtly intense shades of green common to the Workman. They could hear the gentle buzzing of the lights as they flashed in wave after wave across their vision. The water around them bubbled and sparkled as though it were illuminated from within each molecule.

Jack drank some wine and passed the bottle to Natalie, who did the same. They worked on their cigars, the aromatic smoke rising in dense streams straight into the quiet air.

From down the draw a ball of white light flashed briefly then disappeared behind a small cliff before reappearing much closer. Then the pulsing orb raced up towards them, whizzing over their heads and circled the open meadow that surrounded the springs before racing silently back down from where it came. The frogs went quiet with the appearance of the mysterious stranger.

They looked at each other and laughed. Not aliens or their spacecraft. Nothing like that. The coulee contained a peculiar electrical charge that triggered St. Elmo's fire when the humidity and temperature were just right. The ball of heatless flame again tore up the ravine lighting chokecherry trees, pussy willows and curious rock outcroppings in its lunatic light. Then the sphere zoomed right across the surface of the pool between the two of them, flashing past in an unheard, yet perceived "whoosh" before circling and scampering away down the draw.

By now the Northern Lights were so bright everything looked as though it was bathed in the smoothest of green sunrises. The ball of St. Elmo's Fire continued its eccentric orbits. The frogs resumed their croaking, and Jack and Natalie wordlessly enjoyed each other's company and that of the wildly alive Workman Plateau.

~ ~ ~

The next morning Jack was sitting in his attorney's waiting room. The secretary said that Scott "Kid" Camp was running late in his meeting with the two directors of Breezy Sage Development. The nickname "Kid" had something to do with goats during Camp's youth. Jack had never bothered finding out precisely what that might have been. The secretary looked at Jack's swollen, bandaged head and blackening eye, but didn't say a word. Her dour expression spoke for her, like "How tall was the bar stool you fell off of?" Jack stared her down from his sunken position in a well-worn leather chair. He scanned the six-month-old copies of Vanity Fair, ABA Barrister and Dudes & Savages, a yuppie rag if he'd ever seen one. Thousand dollar boots, ridiculous versions of western hats, even more expensive clothes and exorbitantly priced watches and turquoise jewelry. He didn't know anyone who dressed like that, had never seen anyone wear any of those ostentatious items around town, that is until the door to Kid's office opened and out walked a pair of well-tanned men in their early forties. They were wearing those same boots, immaculate over-sized hats adorned with enough pheasant feathers to stuff a pillow, brand new pressed jeans, custom-made western shirts, gold watches, turquoise bracelets and long-cut suede coats.

"We'll take care of the covenants and that little detail on the earnest money, Kid," one of them said with a voice that reflected the arrogance that emanates from those who have more money than they know what to do with and are proud of it, the rest of mankind being merely odious creatures that must be tolerated, barely and preferably at a distance. The pair made money selling nothing but transient enthusiasm and when they'd milked a concept dry, they fabricated another one. 'Money for nothing,' Jack thought. They glanced at him in his faded jeans, worn denim shirt and scuffed boots. Then, just like that, he wasn't there for them anymore. He was not of their kind, so they vanished him from their vision, from their minds. He was trash and proud of it. "See you next week, Kid, when we get back from California."

Kid said "So long," vigorously shook their hands and turned to Jack.

"Boy, what barstool did you tumble off of?"

Jack smiled, painfully. His head hurt despite the two Percodan's Natalie had given him with his morning coffee. They walked into the recently vacated office, the room reeking of expensive cologne, and sat down. Kid easing into a cushy chair behind a large walnut desk cluttered with abstracts, a box of Titleist golf balls, an antique postage scale and yellow legal pads. Jack dropped into a comfortable wingback job on the other side of the huge piece of furniture.

"How in the hell can you represent those clowns?" asked Jack. 'That piece of shit gated community with its ricky-tick, cutesy condos and golf course is going to destroy twenty miles of The Workman. Damn good trout water, not to mention the birds and deer. Now only some rich out-of-state assholes will get to fish it. That is if there are any trout left in it after they get done spraying all those chemicals on the greens. And then we've got to contend with their bullshit around town and a bunch of other crap to boot. Maybe some aging pretty-boy director can make a compelling western movie about a man who dances with golf carts." Jack looked past Kid out the window at people walking along the street. "There's no escaping them. Makes me sick."

"Community needs the money and so do I," said Kid. "They pay well and the development will provide jobs around here, and that's that."

"Yeah and the West sure needs one more golf course. Dumb ass sport. My idea of a dream vacation. Head out to the best country anywhere and chase a little white ball around. Jesus," laughed Jack. Kid wasn't laughing.

The two men stared at each other in silence and Jack thought 'Last time I talk with this sell-out piece of shit and pay for the privilege in the process.'

""Jack, I'll make this short and simple for both our sakes," said Kid as he lit up a Marlboro, exhaling a series of nearly-perfect smoke rings that drifted across the desk. "The wording in your papers is unique to say the least, but the bottom line is your father sold off the mineral rights to Northern High Plains and Dark Star bought them out years ago. Though, you still own the oil and gas rights. From the language I'd have to say that he didn't want you to know about it. Didn't want anyone to know the details until he was dead and buried. Whenever the Consortium decides to dig up the coal on your land, they can. No 'ifs,' 'ands' or 'buts.' They own more of your place than you do. When, if ever, they decide to proceed, they can do pretty much what they want provided they adhere to what passes for environmental regs in Montana. When they're done, they're done and they aren't required to do much in the way of reclamation, of putting back the land the way they found it. Smooth some hills a bit and fill in the holes some. Haul out their machinery and junk. That's about it."

Jack sat in the chair stunned. Nothing to say. His mind reeled at the finality of Kid's words. The realization that his father had lied to him and sold him out, not even that registered. That little item would sink in later after some bourbon. The only thing that ran through his mind was the fact that someday the land he loved, his land, would be torn up, ripped apart and the coal hauled away to be burned for power.

"Nothing you can do?" he asked.

"Nothing anyone can do," said Kid as he stubbed out his cigarette in a marble ashtray. "Sorry to be the bearer of these ill tidings, but I'm not going to waste your money beating a dead horse. All you can do is accept it and move on. It's a tough deal, but the agreements are binding and they're bullet proof. I had a partner look it over and he came to the same conclusion. Your father apparently did the deal with a guy named Bill Foxen. He's a corporate VP for Dark Star. Bill Foxen. I've heard some about him. Tough as nails when it comes to business. Doesn't believe in compromise and knows his stuff. I'll include his contact number in Denver when I send you a breakdown of the deeds and agreements with Northern High Plains that might help clear things up some for you, along with the bill for my time. Check around with other attorneys if you like. Just a waste of money, in my opinion."

Jack looked at Kid, stood up without saying anything or shaking hands, wandered through the waiting room, and out the front door. His feet carried him to that tall bar stool that was waiting for him in the Mint across the street. He ordered a double of Jim Beam and stared at his reflection in the smoky mirror behind the bar. The one Foxen looked into many years ago as had Jack's father many times over the years. A few drinks and a hundred cigarettes later he was still looking vacantly into the mirror when he saw his face transform into that of his father laughing at him, then Natalie's doing the same thing, then once again his father, this time sneering, then the reflection was his own grim, injured self.

"Enough of this shit," Jack muttered. He pushed away from the bar leaving a stack of bills next to his glass and drove back home. The sun was still high in the sky. Mid-afternoon in early May. A long bank of dark clouds was boiling up over the Sanders. The wind was blowing cold out of the west.

~ ~ ~

They began working on the coal hauling rail line on the last day of spring, much sooner than anyone, including Dark Star, expected. Years of political leg work, surveying, spreading a bit of cash in all the right places, a leap in the price of natural gas, especially Canadian gas, crude oil – all these combined to push the process for the granting of right-of-way along the Workman River far ahead of projections. Environmental assessment approvals, even the purchasing of the last few remaining parcels of private land, all of this happened virtually simultaneously. Everything was neatly wrapped up in a couple of frantic weeks in May. Pete Kilduff and the company's legal minions worked long hours to sew up the deals. Jack owned approximately three-hundred yards of land along the planned path of the tracks down by the river. He adamantly refused to sell, no matter what the price. He'd slammed down the phone on Kilduff and refused to meet with the man anywhere or anytime. But when it was discovered that his holdings stopped well short of the water with room to spare on government river corridor holdings, the Consortium made a few minor adjustments and shifted the planned route a little closer to the river and over Jack's little trout stream. The tracks would run across the last few yards of the tiny creek before it joined with the river, but not cross any of his land. Jack's creek would soon be flowing unnaturally through a galvanized steel culvert and pouring into the Workman, like water running from a large faucet.

To say that Jack was angry was an understatement. He saw the proposed line between McCoy and Miles City for what it truly was. One of the last nails in the coffin of a wild Workman Plateau. A now-dead candy bar magnate had bought up miles of the land along the river and sold railroad access for millions of dollars.

Carefully planned and landscaped communities for the well-moneyed, that same group purchasing still other ranches to be run at a loss for tax advantages, plans to pave the country's back roads and on and on. Good country now being brutalized and tamed by men, machinery and greed. Mule deer, Ponderosa forest, a free-flowing river, coyotes, sage grouse, rattlesnakes, turkeys, Jack, Yoter, all of them being exterminated in a relentless miasmic avalanche of technological lust.

"First the fucking train tracks, then what?" he'd say to Natalie or Elmer or anyone else who would listen. "Why the hell not level the bluffs and banks on the west side of the river and build another goddamned golf course. Irrigate the abortion with water from the river. The hell with the catfish, browns, sauger, smallmouths and the game. Hell they could hire Northern Cheyenne from the Reservation for caddies. Nice half-assed western touch for the Californians that would be. 'Hey Lone Wolf, wanna hand me my gap wedge there, chief.' Got to have another golf course, that's for damn sure," and so forth. And his anger would grow and boil and he'd walk the two-plus miles from his home to a cliff overlooking the river and the land where the tracks would be and he'd stare and swear and then, completely frustrated and lost in his rage, he'd scream, a mad, wild sound like the lone wolf he now heard every night sometime after midnight. And he'd start kicking stones and dirt over the precipice and then heave larger stones and then push and strain against boulders lying near the edge, his face purple with the effort, veins bulging along the sides of his head and then he'd cackle madly as the weight of the rock crashed and tore through the survey stakes several hundred feet below him. One day he stopped in the middle of his manic efforts and glanced around at the remaining rocks, some the size of fifty-five-gallon oil drums, and he looked from the path of the proposed rail line far below him and then back at the boulders, and then he laughed silently to himself and said "Why the hell not? What happens, happens." Then he walked back home and drank a lot of whiskey.

Meanwhile, Dark Star went about the business of punching the line through, hopefully before the winter weather, ugly storms screaming down from the arctic, closed in sometime in November. Piles of steel railroad ties, miles of heavy steel track, powerful graders, earth hauling rigs the size of houses, lots of explosives, track-laying machinery, D-11s, all of this stuff began accumulating in the company's yard at McCoy. All of the equipment was painted black with the yellow and red insignias. An evil, sinister army preparing to launch its invasion all along the Workman Front. War. War against the land, the river, the people who lived here, war against a way of life. And Dark Star was planning to win and quickly, too. War all the time.

That last day of spring was miserably wet with dense, filthy grey clouds choking out the sun and drowning the land in a thick, cold drizzle. You couldn't see more than a quarter-mile in any direction. But Dark Star began blasting away at the bluffs and the hills and rock outcrops that blocked the path of the new rail line. And the huge earth haulers belched and roared their way up to the tons of dynamited rubble and sage and splintered Ponderosa and juniper and willow and then hauled the chunks and pieces of the shattered Workman Plateau away to be dumped in the canyon-like pits left from the strip mining over by McCoy. The river ran muddy brown from the work. Greasy slicks of oil, diesel and hydraulic fluid floated on the water's surface reflecting the day's dim light in malignant rainbows.

Jack observed the devastation from a rocky point

far above the insane men and their machinery. He watched in silence. Motionless.

~ ~ ~

One week later, a warm, sunny day, Workman County sheriff Egyptian Healy pulled up in front of Jack's place in his cruiser. He was followed by Pete Kilduff in a Dark Star pickup. The Consortium needed the water on his' land to pump onto the burning seams of coal over at Yoter's. Drilling in on an angle from Elmer's land was proving difficult. The underground water was not where the original soundings had placed it. The liquid appeared to shift and slide all over the underground landscape like an enormous snake. A pair of time-consuming, expensive dry holes had made this clear. The Consortium wanted the water right now and they wanted to begin surveying work on Jack's land, not so much for the coal, but rather as a legal excuse to begin constructing the haul road from Elmer's land through Mad Woman Gulch up the rise past Jack's house and on down the relatively smooth gully where the little trout stream ran. Dark Star could do this. They had all the papers and peripheral legal documentation, but they needed to serve Jack with the action papers to avoid the week or so delay that obtaining a court order would entail. The company was patient, had long-range plans for mining all over this part of Montana and much of Wyoming, but once it decided to move, then that action happened fast. Get on and well into the land before any media-generated news stirred up the hordes of environmental groups waiting out there for a cause, a sexy issue, to hang their nattering, self-righteous hats on. The conservationists, preservationists, environmentalists, whatever they called themselves, Kilduff preferred "posy fuckers," could always be out-spent or out-maneuvered, and as a last resort, out-waited. Everyone in the industry was aware of the fact that most of these crusaders essentially had the attention span of a TV talking head. But Dark Star wanted to get up to speed on this next phase of its southeastern Montana strip-mining operation right now, so they prevailed upon the sheriff to do his duty.

Egyptian Healey, he had family from Cairo, Illinois, hence the nickname, was an old friend of Jack's. They'd gone to school together in the one-room building that sat beside a red dirt road halfway between the Wyoming state line and the county seat of Garland, population 502 and sinking. Jack and Egyptian had hunted together, screwed the same girls in high school, and had more than a few drinks together in the years since. Kilduff knew all of this and figured Healy had at least an outside chance of getting close enough to the obstinate rancher to serve the papers. The sheriff had his doubts and wondered if Jack was as truly outraged as he'd seen him in The Mint recently and heard about from people in Drew and from ranchers out on the plateau. He knew all about Jack's temper. Like the time he'd shot an over-aggressive Kirby Vacuum Cleaner salesman in the foot when the guy had refused to leave at once. The salesman had been forcing himself on every rancher in the county and when Healy turned up an outstanding warrant from Toledo, Ohio concerning the man taking earnest money from people back there for promised aluminum siding jobs that somehow never got much beyond the stage of tacking a square or two of the stuff on the sides of the hapless victims' homes, well, Healy did what needed to be done to protect his friend, an accidental discharge of the 30.30 or something. He also managed to have the Kirby man extradited back to Ohio. Case closed. But that was only one instance of Jack's temper and there'd been a number of others, though he'd been behaving himself ever since he'd started sleeping with that Krietner woman. So Healy was more than a little bit edgy when he pulled up in front of Jack's place and turned off the engine. He left his hat on the seat, checked to make sure his revolver was unstrapped, took off his sunglasses and stepped out of the car. Jack was standing on the back porch steps smiling and holding the 30-30.

"Morning Egyptian. See you dragged some Dark Star scum in your wake," and he levered a round into the gun's chamber. "I'm not talking to him. Said all I want to say to anyone on the matter," and he stepped down to the bottom step.

"Jack, knock it off. I've got to serve you this paper or the court's gonna do the same thing up in Garland. You know how that old fart Thacker is," Healy said with as much calmness and good-neighbor spirit as he could muster, which wasn't much. He was terrified. His shirt was sweat-soaked under his arms and down the back. Jack's eyes were narrowed and his entire bearing was that of a man ready for violence. "Damnit Jack. We've been friends for over forty years and Judge Thacker's only gonna side with Dark Star," and the sheriff jerked a thumb in the black truck's direction. "And he'll probably find a way to fine you some in the process. Hell, he's never gotten over you popping that salesman," and Healy forced a weak laugh.

Graves laughed, too. A mean sound.

"Shit, Egyptian," and he paused and started laughing. "Shit Egyptian. That sounds damn funny to me," and he laughed again, a wild sound that rose in pitch and he began rocking back and forth as he did so. Healy took a step forward.

"Hold it right there," and Jack stepped down to the ground. "Those Dark Star bastards aren't fucking with my land. I don't care if my old man did sell away the rights. And I don't give a rat's ass about the law either, even when it comes dressed up looking like you."

The two men faced off in silence for what seemed like an eternity to Healy, who thought for sure this was his day to die. Jack looked up from Healy to a large raven sitting on top of a tall Ponderosa behind the shed. The bird was motionless but occasionally let out with a grating *cruck, cruck, cruck*, a sound that faded quickly in the stillness. He stared at that bird a long time. Perhaps ten minutes. Then the sheriff thought he detected a shift in Jack's mood. 'A change for the better?' Healy asked himself. 'God, get me out this one and I promise I'll only have six drinks at the bar today. I promise, God.'

Graves took another step and laughed that weird, frightening laugh again.

"Give me your damn paper, Egyptian," and Jack held out his hand. "Come on. I won't shoot you. May shoot that lame fuck in the truck, but not you."

Healy edged forward and thrust the paper to Jack at arm's length while his body uncontrollably leaned in the other direction, towards the perceived shelter of the cruiser. Jack took the document. Shook it open with his free hand, the rifle now clasped in the other and hanging just below his left hip. He read the paper carefully and looked up.

"You're served, Jack ... and ... and ... godda ... goddamnit I'm sorry about this," stammered Healy. "It's all changing 'round here and I ... I hate this goddamned job. Had my fill. No way am I running again."

"Relax, Egyptian. I know," he said calmly. "Go tell that jerk in the truck to come up here. I won't shoot him. If I was up to that, he'd be dead by now. Rumor is the pricks want to pay me for my water to put out that little inferno over on Elmer's. Brain-dead idiots. That coal's been burning forever and my water isn't going to change that any, but if the morons want to pay for the privilege of indulging their absolute stupidity, who am I to stand in their way? My place is history anyway, thanks to the old man." 'And so much for my trout stream,' he thought. 'I'll miss that. Damn all of this.'

Healy looked at Jack and wondered at the change. He'd never in a million years would have imagined that the man would roll over like this. 'He's up to something. I know it, but damn, I just want to get the hell out of here alive,' and the sheriff walked back to the truck, each step an effort in concentration. His shirt was completely soaked with sweat that smelled of fear and stale whiskey.

Kilduff had been taking all this in through the open window of the truck's cab. He looked up at Healy.

"He playing it straight, sheriff or is this a setup?"

"He'd of killed you by now if he was going to, sir. Go on up and say what you've got to say and I'll be there with you. Take it easy and let's just get things settled and get out of here. Okay?"

"That's why we're here, sheriff." Kilduff got out of the black truck and walked up to within ten feet of Jack, who was still holding the rifle in one hand and the order in another. Healy stood to one side and slightly behind Kilduff, right hand on his gun.

"No need for that Egyptian. I hate this asshole and his damn company, but I'm not going up to Deer Lodge for shooting this slime or you either. Hell, a damn head shot wouldn't kill you anyway," and all three men laughed. "Have a seat," and he waved in the direction of an old, weathered table and some chairs gathered on one side of the porch. The ancient bison skull, now cleaned up, was placed in the middle of the round table. "I'll go in and grab some beers and whiskey and don't give me any shit about not drinking while on duty Egyptian. We both know you got enough booze in that car to light up half the Workman," and they all laughed again. The mood seemed almost convivial, but Healy knew better. Jack had never backed down on anything, ever.

He returned with a six-pack of Pabst and a two-thirds-full bottle of Beam.

"Make do without glasses?" asked Jack looking at Kilduff. "Egyptian's like me. A glass just slows down the process," and he cracked a grin in the direction of the sheriff, whose complexion had settled down from purple to merely apoplectic crimson.

"Fine with me, Jack," said Kilduff as he took a drink of whiskey from the offered bottle, then popped the tab on the beer and drained a good bit of it. "That skull looks old. Where'd you find it?"

Jack glanced at the relic and said, "Around here, but let's can the small talk. Get to the point." He looked across to Kilduff who nodded in agreement. A strong acrid, sooty blast from the burning coal over at Elmer's land drifted over the three men. Then a slight breeze worked through the Ponderosa and cleared the air.

"Your father didn't do right by you in my opinion and the company always prefers to do business up front and make everyone happy..."

"Cut the shit, Kilduff. We both know that all you care about is the coal and the money. Leave my old man out of it and make your offer," and Jack took a swig of bourbon, passed the bottle to Healy and lit a smoke, one of Natalie's Newports.

Healy gulped down the whiskey like a man long stranded in the middle of a burning desert and finally being offered a jug of cold water. Then he handed the bottle to Kildiff, who took another drink.

"Business it is," the Dark Star man said. "We need your water to cool things out over on Yoter's place. Should work according to our engineers. And we want

85

to get at that coal now."

"Couldn't steal it from me with that sidewinder drilling act of yours, could you?" said Jack calmly.

"Business is business, and you wouldn't talk with us. We had to act," said Kilduff. He looked at the pack of cigarettes, then at Jack who nodded. Kilduff pulled one out, lit up and inhaled deeply. He exhaled while continuing, the smoke easing out around his words. "We'll give you fifty thousand up front and five-hundred for every million gallons we pump."

Graves looked long and hard at Kilduff, had a sip of whiskey, put out his cigarette and lit another.

"Make it seventy-five and a thousand," he said.

"Done. I'll have the agreement and a certified check for the seventy-five thousand and ten thousand advance on the water we'll use ready in the office tomorrow morning. You can pick it up then."

"Bring all of that here and then we're done," Jack said.

"All right and while we're at it, as you can see from the order, we're going to begin surveying for coal under your land and laying out the haul road, too. If you like we'll route it as far from your place as we can, but work begins tomorrow. You understand?" and it was Kilduff's turn to stare long and hard.

"Yeah, Kilduff. I do. My place is fucked and so am I," said Graves. He took a slash of the booze, handed the remains to Healy, got up and returned with another partially full bottle. "I'm sick of you and your company's bullshit. My coal's down deep. You're not after it right now. You want the haul road for Elmer's coal. Hell, you'll never put those fires out in a million years, but take your best shot," and he laughed quietly. "Guys like you have killed the Workman. Damn good country and you bastards don't know it."

"I understand," said Kilduff as he stood and

indicated that Healy should do the same.

"No. No you don't," said Jack as he stood up and backed away from the table. "Your kind never does and never will," and he looked at Kilduff, who knew enough not to offer his hand. "Bring the papers yourself. There won't be any trouble. My word on that."

"Around nine then," said Kilduff and he got in the truck, backed up and drove away.

Healy was already halfway in the cruiser and he added "Thanks, Jack. All I can say is thanks," and he drove off.

Jack looked back up at the raven on top of the Ponderosa. *Cruck, cruck, cruck.* He picked up the rifle, drew a bead on the black bird and levered round after round until the gun was empty. Pieces of the mangled raven fell through the long needles and plopped on the ground as the noise from the shooting died among the trees. The smell of gunpowder was thick. Some feathers rocked back and forth on the air as they drifted slowly downward.

"Shouldn't have done that," he said to no one. He grabbed the whiskey and went inside.

~ ~ ~

Graves stopped his aged pickup in the dusty turn-around at Elmer's. Part of the exhaust pipe had broken off on the way over, so the old man had heard him coming from a long way off and was outside to greet him. Sixteen curly-haired spaniels. Burnt umber eyes bright with life trooped out the big screened door and with canine dignity down the steps, floppy ears hanging limply at the sides of their heads. Then all of them seated themselves in a semi-circle behind their master. No barking, no wagging tails.

"See your dogs are still at it, Elmer," said Jack, unable completely stifle his laughter.

"Laugh your fool ass off for all I care." Elmer

turned and flicked the well-chewed stub of his cigar over the dogs, ashes and embers raining down on the Boykins. They never moved. "I'm damn near tempted to starve this silent disobedience out of 'em, but I can't bring myself to it. Not yet anyway," and he turned on his dogs. "Not yet, but that day is damn sure coming'. Hear me?" They didn't even twitch a muscle and Jack broke up.

"I know. I know. When you look at it, it's a damn funny situation I've got going' here, but Jesus, this lame-brained behavior ... I just don't know."

"Elmer, those dogs were bred to run. All that energy. You'd think they'd explode after all this time," said Jack as he lit a Camel.

"Well, I'll let you in on a little secret," and Elmer looked behind him at the dogs sitting at attention, all their yellow eyes fixed on the distance of the plateau as the land glided through the orange and purple shades of sunset. He walked up to Jack, leaned forward and spoke in a soft voice. "They don't know this, but I'm on to them. Last few nights I've been sitting up in the dark looking' out by my bedroom window and you know what I saw?"

"No Elmer. What?"

"Not so loud, damnit," and Elmer leaned closer. "Soon as those damned mongrels think I'm asleep, soon as they hear me snoring', they head off the damned porch and run all over the place. I'm not sleeping' mind you. I fake the snoring'."

"Elmer, does any of this strike you as at least a little bit crazy? I mean, you're up in your room in the dark pretending to be asleep to fool your dogs. You might want to look at this situation some."

"Up yours, buddy. This is war and it's been going' on ever since man first began domesticatin' dogs. War. They want to rule the world. Look at them. They think they're some kind of dignitaries and I should be so honored just to be in their high and lordly damn presence," said Elmer, much louder now, but he caught himself, pulled a big green Garcia y Vega cigar from a shirt pocket, bit off one end and torched the thing with his lighter. He turned and exhaled a dense cloud of foul-smelling smoke in the spaniels' direction and yelled "War, you mangy pieces of shit and I'm going' to win. Understand this one right now every goddamn one of you. Me. Elmer Yoter ain't going' to be broken by a bunch of nitwit, pea-brained pieces of shit like you," and he scuffed dirt and gravel in the dogs' direction. Nothing. "Bird season's coming' up and you'd better lose this shit well before then or I'll go out and buy myself a pair of Springers. Now there's a real dog fit for a man."

One of the Boykins blinked an eye. Elmer turned to Jack and said, "See? See that. The oldest one blinked. I'm winning', damnit it. I knew it. I just fuckin' knew it."

"Elmer, one dog blinked in what, two months. Maybe he had something in his eye?" laughed Jack, who was actually a bit concerned for Elmer's mental well being.

"No way Jack. It's a damn sure sign. A break in the wall," roared Elmer as he puffed away on his stogie. He turned back and whispered. "I see 'em through the window and they run and play all night. Round and round the barn, across those fields all the way to the burning' coal and back again. All night when they think I'm out cold."

"Whatever you say, Elmer. They're your dogs," said Graves.

"Come morning' they're sitting on the porch all in a goddamned row, pretty as you please waiting for this old fart to fill their bowls with food," and he walked back over to the dogs, pausing in front of every one of them, long enough to cast a withering stare into the eyes of each Boykin. He stopped, bent over and glared at the oldest one who Elmer called Addison for some unknown reason. The others were nameless. And 'Sure as shit, it did blink' thought Jack. 'Damn shit that goes on around here, nobody would believe me. I'm beginning to think Elmer and those dogs read each other's minds or something.'

Elmer straightened up and flashed a wide grin. "Won't be long now. See what I mean. They're cracking'. When Addison goes, they all will go, and real damn soon, too. Tumble like dominoes, one after the other. Canine mind, even sixteen addled pieces of shit like these all hooked-up together, are no match for me." He tapped his temple with his forefinger and strode into the house.

"I can see that, Elmer," Jack yelled after him. "The intellectual level of energy around here must be similar to what it feels like at Yale. Hell, Oxford."

"Fuck you," and Elmer came out with a bottle of whiskey, the currency of social exchange on the Workman. "Damn fine night. Thought we'd share a little of this out here." Elmer passed the booze to Jack. "Heard that you found out 'bout your father selling the rights. Damn hard piece of news to take, all the way down the line." Elmer looked at his comrade in a way that let him know how bad he thought it was, that he cared, and was with him in this, whatever this turned out to be. The smell of burning coal mingled with sage flavored the evening breeze coming along from the east.

"Thanks, Elmer," and Jack hit the bourbon. "Fucking tore me up and pissed me off. Didn't think Dad would ever do that to me. Always thought he was honest with me about things that mattered. But, what the hell. I was wrong again. Nothing new. And then that Dark Star asshole Kilduff telling me he was going after my coal the other day" ... and he paused and looked up at the sky and all the stars coming out. "Got some money for my water, though. Maybe I'll go down to Mexico, to those mountains Dad and Wimp went to..." and he scuffed a boot in the dirt before asking "You knew about this all along didn't you, Elmer?'

"Yeah, I did," said Elmer as he took the offered bottle from Jack. "Your father never told me, but I knew. Live out here in all this space, all this openness," and he swung his hand around to take in miles and miles of the Workman Plateau, "And you get so damn open yourself that there ain't no such thing as a secret. Drove me crazy when I first realized it, but I learned to live with the madness," and a pack of coyotes howled. "Them damn things not only read minds, they see into the future and they know for good and goddamned sure all hell's going' to break loose around here and I know it, too." Elmer stared off in the direction of the howling that had devolved into a series of barks and coyote cackles.

'You got it all right about everything in this country,' thought Jack as he lit another cigarette.

"Damn straight I do," said Elmer while looking right through Graves. Then he let it go with a cracked, yellowed-tooth smile and passed the whiskey back. "Look, those Dark Star assholes can go pump the entire flaming' Fort Peck Reservoir onto my coal. It'll still be burning' good and goddamned bright from now until doomsday. Only thing that'll stop it is one hell-mad, ball-buster of a storm."

Jack thought 'It's coming. It's coming one way or another. I can feel it, too.'

"Damn straight it's coming'," bellowed Elmer at the sky. "And I wouldn't miss the insane son-of-a-bitch for all the bonded whiskey in Kentucky, buddy. The idiot assholes always say nobody gets outta here alive. Well, that ain't it, damnit. What the goddamned fools are picking at without knowing' it is that no one gets out of here easy. Learn that little fuckin' tune and life ain't so pissin' tough," and he spat out some chewed cigar.

The two men silently shared their friendship and apprehensions in the gathering dark. The coyotes howled and then all was silent. Jack and Elmer drank and smoked without talking.

Then once again that lone, wild, ancient howl rocked across the plateau, a long, deep, terrible moan from the animal he hears every night now and so does Elmer. And all of the Boykins answered as one, a sonorous response to a wildness the dogs shared with the large, lone wolf standing out there somewhere invisible in the dark distance.

Elmer looked at the dogs, then off in the direction of the wolf's call.

"That's what all this goofy shit is about. The dogs. The snakes. The burning' coal. You and Nat screwing by Wimp's grave. All of it. That wolf's the sign."

The dogs were quiet again and motionless. Elmer stood watching the moonrise.

'It's coming' our way, buddy and soon. You and I are in it alone. Nobody else but us and that's it. Together in this mess,' is what Jack imagined he heard inside his head.

"I understand now, Elmer," he said.

"You always did, just takes hard times to bring it out of some of us."

The two men let their gazes wander out over the plateau, now glowing silver beneath the moon.

~ ~ ~

He was rolling down the road between his place

and Elmer's as the sun broke above the plateau. Intense yellow-white light shimmered beside the long dark shadows cast by ancient, eroded volcanic cones rising up from the plateau, the scene further complicated when the brightness was fractured into gleaming slivers and diffuse shadows as it cut through the long needles of the Ponderosas growing next to the road. This panoply of light and dark blurred and burned his whiskey-bloodshot eyes making the high-speed cruise something of an adventure. A thick cloud of dust rose behind the old GMC pickup as it roared along the red dirt road at well over sixty miles per hour. He had the windows cranked down. The cool morning air rushing through the cab soothed his whiskey-ravaged head. Totally lost in the effort it took to keep the pickup from careering into a tree, he failed to notice the flashing red, white and blue lights behind him. The oscillating whining wail of the siren caught his attention, though.

"Fuck," he said while pulling over on a wide spot of the road. The cop car slid to a stop several car lengths behind in a curtain of dust that swept over the truck. He heard its door open and slam shut, then the sound of boots crunching in the dirt. "What now?" he said to himself. "Speeding out here? No way."

In his cracked rear view mirror he watched as several skewed images of the patrolman approached, a tall lean fellow wearing the obligatory aviator sunglasses and a flat, wide-brimmed cop hat. Something looked wrong with the picture to Jack. This took several seconds for the incongruity of the image to register in his Beam-addled mind. This was not a Montana cop. The car had Wyoming markings and the man wore that state's uniform.

"What the hell's going on here?" he said, again to himself as he fished for his driver's license and vehicle registration buried somewhere in his wallet. Did I turn the wrong way coming out of Elmer's and he glanced at the sun rising higher to his right, the east. "Nope. I'm aiming north."

"Morning monsieur. May I see your license (pronounced *leesaunce*), please?' said the Wyoming cop as he stood a few feet from Jack, dark glasses now slipped down to the tip of his nose. A touch of Texas in the guy's voice. West Texas, maybe.

"Here officer." Jack proffered the requisite papers. "What gives? I was only doing sixty."

"Monsieur, the speed limit in Wyoming on unimproved roads is forty-five miles-per-hour or approximately seventy kilometers-per-hour. You were clearly exceeding both these measures of velocity."

'Shit, this fool doesn't even know he's in Montana and what's with this monsieur and kilometer crap?' and he looked at the cop who was a dead ringer for actor Harry Dean Stanton, dark hair and eyes, bony face, sunken cheeks. "Should I say something or what?' and he did, politely pointing out that he'd spent the night at a friend's place four miles back down the road behind him, that this place was two-point-four miles north of the Wyoming line and that they were presently standing six miles into Montana.

"Please look officer, up there at the green mileage indicator over there," suggested Jack and he pointed to a small green sign about a hundred yards ahead of them.

The cop glanced up from Jack's license or leesaunce as the case may be and looked at the sign. Looked at Jack and then back to the mileage marker just as a raven dropped down from the sky and landed on top of it. The bird croaked once and then stared at the two men.

"I appear to have over-stepped my boundaries, here, monsieur. Montana mileage marker number six.

An honest and sincere mistake on my part I assure you. May I give you back your leesaunce and vehicle registration with my heart-felt apologies?" and the cop handed them back and bowed slightly with an ingratiating smile on his face. Jack took them from the man, thought of making a smartass crack and then thought better of it.

"You're not from around here are you, officer?'

"No monsieur. I'm from Paris, Texas."

Jack couldn't hold back on this one and said, "Yeah, I saw the movie."

"Beg your pardon, Monsieur Graves? I don't seem to understand."

"Nothing. Nothing at all," he said. "How'd you end up here?"

"My brother-in-law is a lieutenant with the Wyoming State Police down in Cheyenne at headquarters and he helped me find employment up here. It's a big break for me."

"I can see that," and in his hungover, broken-down condition all of this almost made sense, seemed a part of the normal day-to-day on the Workman. Almost. The confused cop was staring at him with a slightly crazed look that really did remind him of Harry Dean Stanton in that movie, the part at the beginning where he's hoofing it away from everything out along some lonesome rail line. 'Lord,' he thought. 'This life keeps getting weirder and weirder. It just doesn't let up.' He wasn't even going to touch the French accent mingled with the Texas drawl. 'God only knows where this Paris, Texas bullshit will wind up.'

"Monsieur, may I ask you a question, *se vous plais*?'

Jack almost said 'Shoot' but caught himself. "Ask away."

"When I was in Texas I would watch the weather

95

channel on television and it would always show these most horrible storms in Wyoming and Montana. Wind, rain, snow. Most terrible. I've been having the pleasure of working in this beautiful country for three months now and still no storms. Is there a meteorological anomaly occurring in this land? Something I am unaware of?"

'I have no idea what the fuck you're aware of buddy' he thought before saying "No officer," while shaking his head. "Sometimes things blow calm for days on end in this country, then all hell breaks loose, and take my word on it, all hell is going to break loose around here pretty damn soon."

The Wyoming cop thought on this one for a little while then looked back to Jack.

"I think I see now," he said calmly as he pushed his glasses back up the bridge of his nose. "Thank you very much for your time and patience. Again, my most sincere apologies for having interrupted your travels. Good day, monsieur."

"Good day, yourself, officer."

The cop got in his cruiser, turned it around and headed back south in the direction of Wyoming.

"What in the hell is going on around here?" Jack asked himself, then he started up the truck and drove on home. The raven watched him as he disappeared around the bend, then croaked once more and abruptly lifted into the air and vanished itself.

~ ~ ~

He was dead tired when he got home. His joints and muscles ached. He felt perpetually exhausted and he couldn't hold a thought in his head for more than a few seconds. Dizziness was part of his life. The stress from the past few months coupled with the late night with Elmer and his crazy dogs had done him in. He felt better after talking and drinking with the old man. He always did. It was a form of minor salvation to learn that he had a friend who saw things the way he did, the way he'd been trying to deny for years. Yeah he was nuts and yeah, so was Elmer, but so the fuck what? He'd take Elmer's mad loyal friendship to the self-centered superficial phoniness that passed for the real thing these days. He'd take that any time. The way he saw life anymore he figured that pretty much the whole world was insane. Tear up the land, rip out the coal, displace people who lived here for generations and for what? Burn the stuff to generate power to run the tools of ignorance that drove the electronic age that was controlling all of us. That made sense the same way dumping raw sewage in the oceans and rivers did or the Japanese, and us, clear-cutting western Canada and now Siberia. Who needs forests? The whole premise of existence, the lies, the greed, the waste, the posturing social games, all of the ego-centered crap was completely crazy. To pretend otherwise, that was what was insane, to go on pretending that acquiring wildly over=priced pieces of automotive crap – Hey! You want a GPS and video screens in this poorly designed nothingness masquerading as quality? Thousands of acres of land, Persian rugs, Thousand dollar iPads – the ultimate moron gadget, ATVs, snow machines, jet skis, dirt bikes, the NFL and NBA – all this shit meant nothing to him. That was what was truly off the wall. Without value. Not real. Chasing that, the thought of being obsessed with all of the acquisition, that to him was madness, death of the spirit. He wanted none of it. Sharing a nice fire in the middle of nowhere in the still of the night, passing around a bottle and talking some with a good friend like Elmer or Natalie, money couldn't buy it "And thank god for that" he said aloud to the empty kitchen. He poured a little bourbon in a glass, diluted it with some water and drained off the drink while looking out the window. Some black tufts of feathers from the raven he'd murdered the other day were trapped in one of the eye sockets of the bison skull. They quivered at the slightest movement of air. 'Why did I do that? Not like me at all. Kill something for the mean pleasure of it. Not right in the least. Reminded him of when he was a kid with a pellet gun popping innocent creatures. Made him sick to his heart every time he thought of it, and he shook his head and placed the glass in the sink. He pulled off his boots and left them by the table as he did with his shirt and socks. The jeans dropped behind the living room couch as he paused briefly before entering his bedroom. The shades were drawn dimly shutting out the new day. He climbed into bed and Natalie rolled over saying, "I've been waiting for you all night. Where have you been?"

He jumped, surprised at her presence in his bed.

"Damn, girl, you scared the hell out of me. Where's your truck?"

"In the shed. I wanted to surprise you when you got back."

"You sure did that, but you're definitely what I need right now," and he rolled next to her and took her in his arms, pushing the length of his body against her warm, suppleness.

"Judging from the smell of whiskey, my guess is you stayed at Elmer's. Am I right or am I not?" she asked.

"Dead right. Dead, tragically hungover," he said. And then he told her about the Boykins and she laughed. And when he told her about the cop from Wyoming via Paris, Texas she laughed some more.

"You sure Elmer didn't hire the guy as a joke? It sounds like something he'd conjure up to make your day."

"That's always a possibility, but I think not this

time. He's too preoccupied with his damn dogs and the burning coal at this point to plan anything like that," said Jack while reaching over for a cigarette on the bedside table.

"One for me, too," she said.

He lit both of them and handed one to her and placed an ashtray between them.

"The whole thing with the cop was weird, but then everything I have to do with cops is a little twisted. They always fuck with people. A uniform, a gun and those silly glasses, think they're hot shit and can jerk any of us around whenever they want. I'd have no qualms about wasting one of them. One, hell, a whole bunch of the pricks. I hate them all ... well, except for Egyptian. He's okay."

"Easy there big boy," Natalie soothed in a soft voice. "The last time you talked this way, got on one of your anti-cop, anti-control jags, you poured all that sugar and great Vermont maple syrup in the Drew squad cars gas tanks. Maybe it was worth it, but at the expense of that syrup from your friend Myerson. I think not, Jackson."

Whenever she called him Jackson he knew two things. One, she was worried about him and two she wanted to get laid. He didn't like it when she grew frightened or anxious. He did like it when she got "hot" to use her word, so he said, "Just blowing off steam, Nat. Means nothing."

They smoked in silence enjoying each other's company and warmth. She stubbed out her smoke, took his and did the same and then she pulled his head down to her breasts and said "There," in a softly husky voice "Isn't that what you were after when we found that buffalo skull?"

He said nothing, preferring instead to suck her nipples and fondle the warm, furry, moistness between her legs and she sighed, then moaned and climbed on top of him. When they were finished they both fell back on the now damp bed. Eventually Jack got up, opened a window and turned on the small fan on the floor over by the door. Not even nine and already above eighty degrees. He went out to the kitchen and brought back a pitcher of iced tea and two glasses.

They worked on the cold liquid straight from the pitcher and smoked more cigarettes. Then she turned to him and used her long fingers to arouse him again.

"Jesus, Natalie. You trying to kill me off?"

"I need it this morning. I need your cock inside me," and she mounted him once again and began rocking, moaning and fondling her breasts. They continued on working towards their climax and when Natalie came she screamed and looked down at Jack with a glazed, far-away expression and growled "Bill I could fuck you all day. Do things to you ... to you like I did to my father," and her body shuddered again and she cried out "Like my father," and then she collapsed onto Jack's sweaty chest panting. She moaned indistinguishable words.

Jack lay there stunned wondering about what she'd just said, what she may have revealed. Bill. Her father. His stomach felt like he'd just eaten ground glass and his mind was spinning. He tried to sit up and the dizziness drove him back down. Bill. Her father. That's all he could see in his head. He turned his head towards her. She lay on her back with her eyes open staring at the ceiling, at nothing. She was lost someplace else far away. Maybe with Bill. Her father. He wanted to grab her and shake her and yell at her "Who the fuck is Bill? Your father? What did you do to him?" But she was not with him now. Her body was lying next to him, but her head was somewhere else. He managed to sit up. He breathed deeply for a while then stood and staggered naked into the kitchen. He collapsed into a chair at the kitchen table, pulled the bottle of whiskey to him and started drinking. It was nearly full. The bottles always seemed to be full or maybe it always seemed to be empty. Time passed and the whiskey ripped hotly through him and eased the maniacal fire in his head some.

Bill. Her father. Bill. Her father. Over and over and sordid images rose up within him and wrapped around each other growing larger and more perverse. Natalie having sex with two men at once while he watched. Both men were images of her father or actually were her father. One behind her and the other beneath her and the scene grew more elaborate and more perverse and the sickness of it aroused him as he sat naked in the chair, and then disgust replaced the aroused sensation. "Fuck this shit. All of it. Goddamnit!" he yelled. He clutched at the whiskey and lit a cigarette. Bill. Her father. He felt like he was on the edge of something dark and ugly, the genesis of evil within all of us. Was it Bill Foxen, the son-of-a-bitch from Dark Star he'd heard about? He was old enough to be her father. God, was she that sick or turned on by fucking a father look- alike or had she also screwed her old man. He'd never been close to this place before, had never known what real shock and revulsion could do to someone. He was finding out now. The thought of screwing his mother flashed into his mind and he shook his head violently and drove the picture away from him. "Jesus!" He drank from the bottle and the booze slopped out of his mouth, down his chin and onto his naked lap.

Natalie slowly came back to herself and the magnitude of what she'd said while in the grip of her ecstasy overwhelmed her. She'd never said anything to anyone about her affair with her father, about how she'd worn him down with her precocious, sexually active teenage daring and energy – short dresses and flashes of white panties, good-night hugs where she pushed her pelvis hard against him and held herself there until she could feel him growing, and more of the same in not-so-subtle variations. She finally seduced him one night when her mother was out of town visiting her sister. She had wanted to have sex with her father from the moment she began experiencing urges that rapidly progressed to an obsession that she was unable to satisfy with sleeping with her older male classmates and men twice her age. Her father had noticed her maturing body for some time and, despite his best efforts at prayer and pushing away the sexual thoughts and fantasies he had for her, he was losing the battle. What took place between them was as inevitable as it was forbidden in their society. She came down still damp from her shower wearing only her bra and panties. She'd acted surprised to find him home, but she walked up to him with a most womanly smile and he tumbled, grabbing her and fondling her while she worked at getting his pants off. From there they progressed to the carpet and then he entered her with one hard stroke and then the two of them were lost in each other. The orgasms she had with her father were like no other she'd ever experience again in life, though she searched relentlessly for the man who could bring her to that point of physical hysteria and at the same time bring her emotional security. The danger and thrill of the illicit nature of having sex with her father could never again be duplicated. Her relations with Jack and with Foxen had come the closest. Jack because of his stamina and drive along with his physical and emotional similarity to her father. Foxen was seventy and offered her the obvious older, wiser man image and he was gentle, attentive and finally submissive as her father had been for those blissful few months back when she was fifteen. Both men did whatever she asked and they tolerated her teasing and evasions. She loved driving both of them mad with their lusts and frustrations. The ride with her father had all come to a horrible end when their mother discovered the two of them in bed one afternoon when she'd returned early from a Saturday shopping spree. Rage, guilt and sorrow filled the house for weeks that never seemed to move through time. A nightmare that ran forever. No one spoke to anyone except in either mumbled, short sentences or when the tension became so unbearable, curse-filled screaming filled the house to the delight of their nosy neighbors. Things continued to worsen. Natalie was exiled to a private girls' school in Michigan and her mother refused to even discuss a divorce. She wanted to put her husband through hell and beyond if that was in any way possible until the day he died. He had paid for every remaining second of his life. A month after she went away to school her father was found dead in his study, the insides of his head splattered in a mess of exploded bone, blood and brains all over the walls and curtained windows. Guilt and his army Colt .45 were the culprits. Her mother swiftly unraveled to the point of perpetual incoherency and unstoppable tears and screaming fits of rage, finally winding up in an expensive institution out in Topeka, Kansas. From that moment on, from the day her mother disappeared inside that facility, Natalie had done everything she could to put the affair far behind her, including changing her name and moving out west to Montana. Now in this obscure, isolated part of the world, the Workman Plateau, her relationship with Jack and her affair with Foxen had brought all of the memories of that time back as though they were happening right now, and worse she had gone a long way towards exposing herself to others by saying what she had while fucking Jack. And to make matters worse, she was also screwing the man who had conned Jack's father out of his mineral rights and was now in charge of destroying his land.

"God! What have I done?" she said to herself and the empty bedroom while pulling on her jeans and shirt. "What can I ever say to Jack?" and she knew that once again she had done something horrible, almost unspeakable, to a man she loved.

She found him still sitting naked at the kitchen table with a bottle of Jim Beam in front of him and a smoldering cigarette burning a deep scar into the wood finish. Perspiration was beaded on his forehead. The room stank of cigarette smoke, whiskey and the sweat of despondency. He looked up at her with bloodshot eyes and then took a long drink from the bottle. She went out and picked up his jeans in the next room and grabbed his shirt from the floor.

Put these on, babe," she commanded gently and he did as she asked before slumping back into the chair again.

"How could you ... Foxen ... your father," he said in a voice that wasn't his, something that sounded like it was coming from an open grave. He stared at the table for a long time. She waited him out. "Whore. Bitch. Cunt. Slut," and he laughed darkly to himself, then fixed her with a stare of hate that tore down through her. "Any names I missed? Hate to short-change you on this one after all of your efforts ... it's all some damn con isn't it? You fucking any man you see, my old man fucking me and Dark Star fucking my land ... Well ... Fuck you, too." He laughed morosely, had some more whiskey, dropped his cigarette on the floor and ground it out with his bare heel. He lit another. "Fucked your old man. That's sick. And Foxen. What was I to you, just some asshole to play games with?"

"Jack, that happened a long time ago and the thing with Bill was almost over. A mistake," she pleaded. "It's you I want to be with. I know I've lied and done horrible things ... I ... I just couldn't stop myself," and she began to cry. "I am a bitch and all those other things you said. Goddamnit, I'm sorry to have done this to you and ..."

Jack cut her off with another "Fuck you. Listen you bitch, I don't ever want to see your perverted ass around here again. You make me sick and I'd like to blow your fucking head off. Get the goddamned picture, Natalie?" and the two were silent. A pair of magpies made up for this gap with a loud argument over something of avian value lying below the Ponderosa over by the shed. He looked out the kitchen door and saw another raven sitting atop the tree. "I knew I shouldn't have shot you the other day. Bad luck all the way. What a dumb shit." He drank more bourbon, ground the smoke out with his other heel and lit another.

"We've all sold our souls," he said.

"That's why we're here," she said. "That's why we're here."

He nodded and went back to the whiskey. She got up and left.

·THREE·

"Life goin' nowhere, somebody help me. Somebody help me, yeah." Would this never end, he asked the scorched pavement beneath his burning feet? Where does all of this come from? The infernal and apparently eternal heat and thirst were penance enough, but to have a song by the BeeGees rattling around in his head was beyond the pale. Life was unbearable as he wandered this mean, desolate, heartless alley all the while not gaining any ground. He was standing in place while moving his feet as fast as he could. There was no one anywhere to be seen. He knew where he was but he was lost without hope of finding his way, let alone gaining even the slightest of redemption from a life filled with mistakes and all too often, self-interest bordering on infantile narcissism. Under cloudless a sky and a brutal sun, the harsh white light turned his surroundings into a monochrome glare. Coiled snakes were backed up against garbage bins and discarded, filthy mattresses. They hissed at him as he passed by without going anyplace. "What's new?" he said aloud, the sound of his voice dying in the stillness. A deep purple thunderhead appeared instantly overhead from somewhere and drenched him with cool rain. Lightning and thunder flashed and pounded through the alley blinding and hammering at his senses. Then the storm vanished and sunlight returned. At his feet now was an open Styrofoam cooler filled with ice and

Molson's Ale. He stopped trying to walk, reached into the cooler for a bottle, twisted off the cap and drank, the cool liquid. This revived him. He had another bottle and still another. Then he heard Radiohead playing from its King of Limbs album – "I think I have had my fill (Don't hurt me)... I think I should give up the ghost (Don't hurt me)." Up ahead an enormous moose, its rack the width of a billiard table, stood in the opening between the buildings at an edge where the alley gave way to a cross street. He opened another bottle of beer and started walking for real...

~ ~ ~

The five-foot snake struck from its coiled position next to the pile of steel railroad ties that were stacked at the end of the newly laid tracks. The construction worker was inspecting the ties for damage that may have occurred when they were off-loaded the other day. The rattlesnake's head struck out, its mouth closed, then swiftly it opened wide, the inside white and lined with a dozen or more needle-like teeth. The force of the reptile's unleashed muscles drove the large inwardly-curved fangs through the man's pants just above the tops of his work boots, sinking the hollow points into the calf muscle, releasing their venom and withdrawing, mouth closed once again, all of this in an instant. The punctures felt like someone had driven a pair of large cactus spines into the worker's flesh and he screamed, stumbled and fell next to the ties. Several smaller snakes lay coiled in the shadows and they, too, lashed out, razor-sharp fangs piercing the man's arm, his larynx and his right eye. The rattlers slithered away to the shelter of some crumbling rock nearby. The extreme dose of venom circulated swiftly through the man's body, within minutes causing an overwhelming sense of giddiness like a cheap Benzedrine rush. This was followed by a pervading feeling of weakness and numbness bordering on paralysis. The bite areas began to swell and turn bright red with smudges of purple. The man, now lying on his side in the dirt, vomited on his arm and hands. His pulse became feeble and erratic. His blood pressure plummeted. Within twenty minutes he was dead.

There was no one around to see this happen. He was out here alone making the inspection on a Sunday afternoon, the one day Dark Star employees and various other sub-contractors took off. The punching through of the rail line along the Workman was not yet halfway completed and it was already mid-August. The crews were far behind schedule because of the earlier accidents: the two men killed by a slab of sandstone that sheared from a cliff a few miles back up the tracks, then the machinery sloughing off into the river when an underground trickle of water decided to become a full-fledged spring and turn the ground around the rail bed into quicksand. And cold, blustery weather would be dropping down from northern Canada soon. The worker's body cooled following death as it lay there in the paling orange light of the setting sun. Ants, wasps and beetles were already at work devouring the man's flesh. They crawled through his mouth, down his throat and began chewing on his stomach and intestines. Others nibbled and munched through his eyes and bored into his brain. An insect banquet high on the Workman.

Kilduff was on the scene by 5:35 the next morning, as soon as he got the call from the first crews to show up for work. The body was a mess. The insects had made serious headway, leaving oozing trails in the man's skin. Coyotes had gnawed away at his face and fingers and apparently a much larger animal had ripped open the dead man's stomach, tearing out the skin and muscles in one large bite. Whatever the animal was, it had left a slimy string of dead man's intestines looped over the pile of metal ties. The pile of guts were already covered with flies. The ropy mess hummed and buzzed an iridescent blue-green as the early morning light played off the bugs. Huge tracks, the size of both a man's hands pressed into the ground with great force led across the rocky soil before disappearing at the edge of a sandstone escarpment.

"Holt shit," said Kilduff. He had seen his share of gruesome deaths over the years, bodies smashed to pulp by cave-ins, blown apart by explosions, mangled by machinery accidents, but this corpse was the worst. Already beginning to bloat, savaged by the animals and insects along with the expression of abject horror on what was left of the face. Lips chewed away, tobacco-stained teeth opened wide in a rictus grin of agonized death. There was a dried, cloudy yellow discharge from the suppurating wounds caused by the snakes. The eyes were gone leaving dried, withered sockets.

"Never seen anything worse," he said to the men gathered around the body. He turned away, coughed and spit up the morning's coffee, wiped his mouth on a shirtsleeve and turned back. "Never heard of animals eating a carcass that's been killed by rattlesnakes. When's the damn coroner get here?"

"He called on his truck phone and said he'd be down from Garland by 6:30. An ambulance is coming with him."

This was now the third accident. Kilduff was concerned, both for his men and about completing the line before winter. He'd never missed a deadline, but then he'd never had to contend with any of this before. And, god, the size of those tracks. The dog, coyote or whatever must weigh at least two-hundred pounds. He'd seen Irish Wolfhounds, Newfoundlands and Mastiffs that size, but never coyotes or even wolves. It wasn't possible. The last of the buffalo wolves had been trapped out of this country decades ago, and the way these tracks vanished into nothingness at the base of that rock wall, the situation was like some kind of northern high plains voodoo.

"What the hell gives here?" he wondered.

"How's that, boss?" asked his foreman.

"Oh nothing, Jim. Just thinking out loud," and he looked at the other man. "How the men taking this? Any trouble you see brewing?"

"Couple of 'em puked when they saw the body or what's left of it. Few more grumbled about shit work and bad luck on the job, but that's about it. Nothing I wouldn't expect to hear under the circumstances," and the foreman paused and stared at the river flowing muddy and oily a few yards away. "I can handle it boss. Worked with most of the men over at McCoy and down in Wyoming. They trust me and will do what I say. It's okay."

"Glad to hear it," said Kilduff with a nod. "I've got to get back and call Foxen. Let me know if there are any snags with the coroner." He looked at the river and wondered what was going to happen next. "I'm going to ask Foxen if we can go seven days a week. And I'll work out an incentive bonus for the men, but keep quiet on that for now."

"No problem," said the foreman but before he could continue, the ear-splitting noise of large rocks crashing down the cliff echoed through the river canyon. All this sounded like a mortar attack to Kilduff, reminding him of battles he'd barely survived over in Iraq quarter-of-a-century ago.

Boulders the size of garbage cans bounced and crashed off the pile of broken rock at the base of the cliff then caromed into a flat car loaded with steel rails. The stone exploded like bombs, shards of rock whistling through the air, clanging into the machinery and tearing into the men. Fingers, hands, torsos and legs were torn into bloody, ragged pieces. It was all over in seconds. Men were screaming, moaning or lying on the ground unconscious or dead. It looked like a combat zone. Yellow-green dust filled the air.

Kilduff's left arm was bleeding, the skin ripped just below the elbow by a sharp hunk of rock. His foreman was lying on the ground at his feet, blood bubbling around the edges of a spear-shaped piece of stone embedded in his skull. Others staggered around bleeding, clothes shredded and in shock. The ones who were not hurt either ran to help their injured comrades or were fleeing for their lives back up the tracks or leaping into the river and swimming desperately for the opposite bank of the Workman River.

Kilduff raced over to his truck, punched in 911 and yelled "There's been a major accident on the Workman rail project, mile thirty-six. Men have been killed or are seriously injured. Send every ambulance and emergency vehicle you've got."

"This is the Drew 911 emergency line, can you repeat the location and nature of the injuries?" a flat voice over the phone asked.

"Men are dead at mile thirty-six on the Workman rail project, goddamnit! Send mother-fucking help now. Right now," and Kilduff was screaming into the receiver.

He looked around. Wounded men, comatose men, dead men were scattered about the work site, bodies draped and slumped at grotesque angles all over the work site. Wails of pain and terror sliced through the air. Kilduff thought he could taste the salty, metallic flavor of blood on his tongue along with the dusty, gritty feel of slate and sandstone. The rail car had been knocked off the tracks and was resting on its side. The rails were scattered down the bank. Some were partially submerged in the greasy, brown water. He looked up at the place where the boulders had come from. Nothing. No sign of anyone or anything that might have caused all of this. He followed the avalanche's course down the cliff, bright scrapes and impact marks scarred the several-hundred-foot rock face that consisted of striations of slate, coal, sandstone and jagged rips of clinker.

Several hundred feet above the top of the cliff three ravens glided on the morning breeze riding the air toward the distant Sanders Mountains that flashed purple, coral, and white in the angled light of the rising sun.

Above the cries of his men's agony Kilduff thought he heard sounds of laughter coming from beyond the edge of the escarpment. Mad, insane voices that drifted just barely into his hearing, then vanished, then flickered back to him again. Inhuman sounds. Weird. Or perhaps it was only a distant pack of coyotes barking and howling. Could be grasshoppers clacking through the warming air. Then again, maybe it was the wind talking through the grass. The morning breeze died away and with it the laughter.

The ravens cackled as they flew over the devastation below them.

Cruk, cruk, cruk.

They soared on wide, black wings over the cliff across the river, the birds becoming smaller and smaller shapes, dark pinpoints against the blue. Then they were gone.

~ ~ ~

Jack bounced around on the padded, spring-loaded seat of the old John Deere tractor that had done the fieldwork on the ranch for more years than he could remember. He'd picked the machine up for a song over in Ekalaka one day while over there hunting pheasants not far from the Chalk Buttes. The machine was sitting out in front of a service station with a "For Sale" sign on it. He had paid $625, then driven home, hooked up his trailer and lugged the thing back to the ranch. Since then the dependable machine had plowed fields for wheat, cut hay, pulled stumps, spread manure, and, as it was doing on this hot, blue sky morning, pulling a baler that was almost as old as itself and literally held together with baling wire. The whole works rattled, wheezed and clattered over the rough ground. Occasional puffs of blue-black smoke belched from the exhaust, an indication that the engine needed another ring job. One more winter maintenance chore. Clouds of grasshoppers flew up in front of the tractor like crested water alongside the bow of a cruise ship slicing through the ocean. The hoppers flew past Jack in a steady stream, bounced off his face and arms, and sailed by the baler. He worked back and forth in a steady rhythm across the one-hundred-plus acre field that ran along the base of a limestone bluff on one side and a small but steady stream that wound around the rest of the perimeter in an exaggerated and serpentine C. The added moisture from the creek made this the best hay producing land he had. Jack counted on this hay to help get his cows through the long winters. Sometimes, in what passed for moist years on the Workman, he got three cuttings, though the third was always a bit on the slim side. This year looked like two, he thought as he watched the rectangular bales spew from the rear of the baler every 10 yards and land in the stubble. An old Bobby Watson tune played in his head. Complex Dialogue it was called. Watson on alto sax and his great sideman, Terell Stafford, on trumpet. The two, now expatriates making a go of it in Milan, Italy because this country didn't support its jazzmen worth beans, riffed back and forth in Jack's head. It was a remarkable piece of elaborate music that the two men executed with such confidence and flare that it sounded pure and simple. As Jack and the machinery droned up and down the field in the growing heat, a slight movement in the trees along the base of the limestone cliff caught his eye. At first he figured it was a mule deer working towards a cut in the rock, then he figured it was one of Coaker's mastiffs because of the animal's short legs. He caught one more ghosting flash of it, noticed a long, bushy tail and that the overall color of the creature was a gray-buff. Not a mastiff with that tail and shading, he thought. He wiped his eyes on his shirtsleeve and looked again. Nothing. Whatever he'd seen was gone.

"Probably one of Coaker's dogs," he said to himself. "Damn heat's playing tricks with my eyes," and he continued baling hay.

~ ~ ~

Through his telescope Elmer could see two large pipes pouring water into the jagged tear in the baked ground and down onto the burning coal, the place not far from where the Dark Star truck was swallowed whole last spring. The pipes were twelve inches in diameter. They delivered thousands of gallons per minute that gushed and sprayed onto the inferno. Sooty steam shot far above the land, the vaporized liquid billowing from the fissure in whirling, hissing clouds. The crew had been pumping this water into the crack in the earth for three days now with some results. They worked continually. At night beneath the billion stars, huge arc lights illuminated the scene with surreal intensity, the harsh white light throwing long, black, almost alien shapes that mirrored the actions of the men as they went about their business. Nothing like this shadow play had ever been seen on the plateau before. Every twenty-four hours they moved the pipes a hundred feet along the fault believing that they'd put out a section of the red-hot coal, but Elmer doubted if the seams were any more than temporarily cooled down, waiting to flare up once again as the bituminous coal dried in the intense heat of the adjacent flames and red-hot embers. A downdraft of oxygen, a spark or two, and wham, things would be back to the usual simmering, smoking belching routine.

"Damn fools never will get the thing out," he muttered to the Boykins that were either sitting next to Elmer or lying supinely on the ground paws splayed, bellies taking in the noon sun. "Tore all hell out of Jack's place putting in that goddamn well and haul road and for what? A dumb-ass steam bath. Fools, every one of them, I tell ya. All that water those idiots are usin' will make Jack rich, yet," and Addison wagged his tail and yowled in agreement. Elmer and the Boykins were on speaking terms once again following the night with Jack that featured the lone wolf's howl. No more silent treatment from his spaniels. No more military rigidity. The dogs were their normal, undisciplined selves again and Elmer, though he'd never admit to this, was relieved. He'd secretly feared that his Boykins' silent treatment would finally wear him out and that he'd have to admit as much to them, a humiliation he was not prepared to face.

Elmer had not seen his friend in a while, ever since this latest disaster along the Workman rail line. Graves had pulled up in a cloud of dust as soon as he'd found out about the accident and given Elmer the lowdown before saying he had to run up to Miles City to pick up some supplies, fencing material, window screening and, of course, a few cases of Jim Beam. He promised to get a few boxes of cigars for Elmer at the smoke shop down on Main. That was a week ago. Elmer figured

Jack was holed up at Chambers Point shooting his guns, drinking whiskey and swearing at the sky. Letting off steam, just like the land was out by those big pipes.

Rattlesnakes had killed one man and three others died in the avalanche by the river. Several more had been badly injured. One man lost a leg. Another had his spinal cord damaged and would be paralyzed for life, and still another was blinded by the shale shrapnel. But the track laying went on, now seven days a week around the clock.

"Serves the dipshits right," Elmer said to Addison who blinked his yellow eyes in agreement. "Don't like to see people hurt, but they're messing with our land and our way of life," and Addison barked once. The other dogs turned their heads or rolled over and looked in his direction.

Dark Star and Kilduff had gone out of their way to route the haul road from Elmer's conflagration to the Workman as far from Jacks' place as possible. Aside from the fact that this turned out to be the most cost efficient location, Kilduff wanted to keep as much distance from Jack's raging path as possible. He figured the man was on a long-term, slow burn that could ignite at any moment at the slightest provocation. Gunfire and worse was entirely possible the way Kilduff saw things. They'd even placed the well far behind a thick stand of Ponderosa back down a hill and out of sight of the house. Not the best location, but workable. The twin pipes ran parallel to the graveled road and the noise from the huge trucks moving and dumping aggregate to beef up the byway vibrated for miles across the open sage flats and brushy coulees. No more peaceful, silent nights. No more game, either. The mule deer and white tails had vanished as had the sage grouse and turkeys. Dark Star had completed all of this work in less than a month – the road, the well and pumping station, and the pipelines.

The well tapped into the aquifer which probably contained trillions of gallons of water that had trickled and filtered down through the porous ground over thousands of years – rain, sleet, snowmelt – and was now being wasted away on an unstoppable subterranean fire. The aquifer fed the hundreds of springs that trickled and poured life-giving water out across the plateau. When it was used up, thousands of acres of the country would turn barren, lifeless. The only good thing, if that was indeed the proper word, was the fact that Jack's trout stream was still flowing, perhaps even a little stronger than before the drilling. Jack told Elmer before he left for Miles City, that his brown trout were doing fine, but that "the savages had ruined the lower mile of the creek when they put in the haul road." Culverts, mud and rock, oil spills, the works. But the hyper-strain of brown trout had come through the ordeal like pros. The majority of the fish had moved into the upper stretch by his house when the construction began. That two miles or so of willow and alder lined stream probably had three-thousand trout swimming around and nudging each other for prime holding areas and scrambling for every mayfly, caddis and grasshopper in sight. The incredible number of fish probably made it "one of the finest trout waters in Montana," said Jack with a wry grin and a flip of the finger towards McCoy and the Consortium's headquarters.

One of the many downsides to all of the construction was the sound of the industrial pump running night and day, a constant visceral drone that wiped out the awesome stillness of the land. Elmer hated the noise and had caught himself more than once clutching one of his hunting rifles, or his .357 or even found himself staring through one of his rifle's scopes sighting in on a member of the water crew. He usually did this at night when things seemed more intriguing to his mind. "Sort a like jack lighting deer," he'd whisper to the dogs."

But soon enough he'd pull off the rifle.

"No way, Elmer, you old fart," he'd growl to himself. "Not yet anyway." He was having a high old time smoking his cigars and drinking whiskey while observing the futile efforts of what he liked to call "those numb-nuts bastards from the Consortium." Elmer liked the way the word consortium rolled around in his mouth. "Consortium. Consortium. Consortium" he'd singsong to some nameless tune of his own creation.

Elmer took a slug of whiskey and a big puff on his cheap, green cigar then turned back to the telescope just in time to see men running away from the steaming crack in the ground. He adjusted the focus and zeroed in on the rip in the ground, which was rapidly growing wider, large sheets and chunks of ground were sliding into the now gaping hole like they were being funneled into the maw on a gigantic conveyor. Steam and thick smoke obscured the men as they piled in their black trucks and tore away from the death trap in reverse, wheels spinning as they tried to gain purchase on the loose, sandy ground. Chunks of dead sage and cactus plants spun beneath the burning tires and got tangled in drive trains, exhaust systems and axles. The wind carried sounds of the crew screaming and swearing, the human noise distorted and feathered by distance, and Elmer could smell the smoking tires and burning clutches, acrid, greasy scents.

Then an explosion rocked the area with a force that rippled across the land, the concussion of the blast wave knocked Elmer off his feet, blew his hat from his head and thoroughly upset the sixteen Boykins who began howling and barking at everything in general while running and leaping in frantic circles. The ground actually rose in a humping wave a couple of feet high, rocking his home and busting out most of the windows. The back door was wrenched from its hinges.

Elmer struggled to his feet and what he saw, well he didn't need a telescope to view the intense orange fireball unfolding more than a thousand feet above him. Pieces of rock and dirt began raining down on Elmer and the dogs. It pounded on his metal silo in sharp pings and loud bangs. A fine dark-gray ash started falling down on all of them like perverted snow. The Boykins yipped and snapped as some of the rock nailed them. They looked up angrily at the sky and howled, eyes flashing with anger at the unexplained attack.

"I could of told 'em, the dumb shits," Elmer lectured to the whirling spaniels. A rock the size of a marble bounced off his head. "Ouch. That bastard hurt," he yelled as he rubbed the spot of impact. "That coal can't be put out by men and their machines. Most likely a ton of flammable gas mixed in that big ole hole, too. I bet one good goddamn dollar that the shit re-ignited all at once and went 'Kaplooee.' That's all she wrote. Good damn night Irene."

He set up the telescope, also knocked over by the blast, readjusted the focus and searched for the Dark Star trucks. He spotted two of them three miles away weaving and sliding up the haul road on the far side of Mad Woman Gulch. The pickups were running at a dangerous speed, a thick cloud of red dust trailing behind. He scanned the horizon for the other truck. Nothing. Then he panned near the source of the still-climbing mushroom cloud. The hole in the ground was now as wide as a football field. Sparks, flames, ash, rocks, sage brush, weathered juniper, long-dead

Ponderosa stumps and limbs, all sorts of stuff, were soaring into the air like some berserk fountain. Swinging the scope slowly to his left he picked out the other wrecked pickup more than one-hundred yards from the blast site. Nose down and crumpled like an accordion, windshield and all the other glass smashed out. The explosion must have heaved the truck a couple of hundred feet in the air before it crashed into the parched, rock-hard soil nose first. Elmer zeroed in on the cab, at least what he could see of it. A bloody mess. Both men were mangled, severed limbs lying on the ground in front of the crumpled hood. The old man almost threw-up, but a pull of whiskey controlled the situation.

"Hell of a bad way to go," he said to Addison, now standing next to him. The other dogs were arranged in their customary semi-circle behind them. "Hell of a way to die."

The man and his dogs stared out across the fiery Workman Plateau and watched as the mushroom cloud kept rising and rising.

~ ~ ~

The evening of the explosion Kilduff called Foxen down in Denver. It seemed like all he'd been doing for the past couple of weeks was talking with his boss. The first two deaths along the rail line, the damaged equipment, the man killed by the rattlesnake, then the three others and now this. The damn media was all over the story, hanging around the bars and restaurants in Drew, outside the McCoy work site, the Workman River site and on the fringes of the Yoter place. Several reporters and cameramen had tried to approach the old man, but he'd driven them away with rifle and pistol fire, not to mention that pack of dogs of his. Dragged down one guy from CNN. Let him go and turned on his camera.

Kilduff got Foxen's secretary, who he knew well, He succinctly briefed her on the situation while she tracked down her boss on another line.

"What a zoo Yoter's got going. Hell, what a zoo I've got going. We need to pull off this job right now. Drop the whole thing. Make a big environmental sob story pitch and cut our losses. We're losing men and I can't comfortably live with that. Never had shit like this happen before. And we're millions of dollars over budget already. Yoter's coal is a damn sinkhole. Hope the old man goes for jumping ship on this one. Always listened to me in the past. He damn well better this time."

"He might," she said. "But I've never seen him this worked up or focused before. He's on the line now. Good luck," and one connection died and another clicked to life.

"Pete. I already got the news. It's been flashed on network TV," said Foxen in a loud, angry voice. "Saw it on CNN. Jesus, those dogs did a number on that camera guy. What in the name of hell you boys got goin' up there?"

Kilduff filled him in on the latest tragedy, that even though there was a feel of sabotage to the some of the mayhem, that there were no clear signs of outside interference. Kilduff also informed Foxen that six of his best men had quit not only the job, but Dark Star completely, and more were threatening to do the same. That environmental groups were starting to get their poor, little febrile imaginations all worked up. He went on to describe his ideas on how Dark Star could pull out of this without any further damage, maybe even get some good PR. Donate money to the various environmental groups in the region, set up trust funds for the dead men's families and clean up the haul road and Workman River.

"No way!" yelled Foxen. Kilduff held the receiver away from his ear. "We never quit on a course of action we've already begun, that we're committed to. That's policy. Carved in stone. No way. The trust funds – Yes. The other crap – Never!"

"But Bill..." Kilduff started.

"No. Period. Got it?"

"Yes, but it's a mistake."

"Screw the mistakes, Pete. I'll fly up there in the morning and we'll straighten things out.

"See you at the airport."

The line went dead with a loud click.

Kilduff looked at the phone and wondered what would happen next.

"We're all going to be screwed major on this one," he said to no one but himself.

He stood up and looked out the window to the Workman Plateau simmering under the brutal August sun that seemed to hang motionless in a cloudless sky that was burned from blue to a searing white. Miles away he could see coal smoke drifting across the barren, burned out land on Yoter's place.

"I can feel it. We're history," he said to the view stretched out before him.

~ ~ ~

Coaker Triplett's two mastiffs were on the trail of a crippled mule deer. The pair had probably run down more game on the Workman than Jack, Elmer and Coaker had shot in a lifetime. Most of the area's residents considered the dogs a menace and both dogs had the scars along their flanks from buckshot and bullets to prove it. The dogs weighed over two-hundred pounds each. They'd drop their squared heads down to the ground to check the scent of the deer, the dogs' large, drooping ears dragging in the dust. And then off they'd go again, thick paws pounding the ground as they loped along, relentlessly closing distance on their prey, an animal with three good legs and one badly ripped one that had been tangled and then torn in some discarded, rusty barbwire from a fence Dark Star had ripped up while laying the haul road. The mastiffs came up over a small hill and spotted the panicked deer hobbling down a steep cut on the edge of Mad Woman Gulch. The mule deer was desperately trying to reach the sheltering tangle of brush and grass at the bottom of the coulee. The buck knew his way through the tight, tunnel-like game trails that wound back and forth along the bottom of the gulch. The dogs broke into a run, saliva dripping from the corners of their mouths, big white teeth glinting in the sun. The deer stumbled over an exposed tree root, lost its footing and rolled up against the gray hulk of a dead Ponderosa. The animal struggled to regain its feet. The mastiffs, slobbering jaws agape, lunged for the throat and exposed belly of the deer.

Neither of the killers reached their prey.

Something larger than the two mastiffs roared as it leapt from its vantage point on top of a flat outcropping of sandstone above the deer. The creature flew down the slope covering the forty feet between the rock and the dogs in one leap. It was the lone wolf and it had been tracking Coaker's hounds for a week now, always keeping the breeze at the right angle, blowing from the dogs to it so that the mastiffs never winded the large carnivore. The wolf crashed into one of the mastiffs, driving it into the other one. Both dogs were knocked down to the bottom of the gulch. The wolf was right behind them. As soon as it regained its balance, the predator nearly tore the head off one mastiff with a powerful swipe of its huge teeth, then it swung on the other mastiff and ripped its belly open from hind legs to chest. Both of Coaker's dogs lay on the ground. Blood sprayed in the hot air, splattered all over the brush and ground, and pooled beneath the bodies. The disemboweled mastiff weakly lifted its head, life's light fading from its brown eyes. It tried to lick at the tear in its belly but died while doing so, the heavy head falling back in the dirt with a thump.

The wolf shook itself, fluffing and rearranging its fur, blood and pieces of guts shooting in a wide arc. The animal looked at the kills, then let loose with the howl of a natural born killer, a sound that swept up out of Mad Woman Gulch, cut across the Workman Plateau and roared across the sage flats. The wolf then moved to the damaged mule deer, which was now waiting for doom to come its way. Both animals, breathing heavily from their exertions and the presence of death, stared at each other. The wolf approached the deer. The predator crouched low to the ground, then leapt and crashed down on the head of the frightened animal, breaking its neck as it did so. The wolf began tearing away chunks of the dead deer's flesh.

From its vantage point on a tree limb thirty feet above the place of the ambush a small puma watched the curious drama. The cat was morphologically closer to the long-extinct American Cheetah than the present-day cougar, but then, who's really keeping accurate track at the moment. The smell of blood and killing was thick in its nostrils. The fur on the cat's back stood up. The puma had also been tracking the deer, but was keeping well away from the mastiffs. When the wolf was gone, the panther dropped to the ground and pounced on the deer, ripping out its jugular. The cat tore at the warm flesh, eating its fill before dragging the mangled remains of the carcass into the brush. The kill was covered with grass, sticks and dirt. The cat marked the place with its urine, a warning to other animals to keep away. Then the puma climbed back up to its limb, cleaned itself and dozed in the heat of the day.

~ ~ ~

Jack and Elmer had been going at it for nearly six hours, since before sunrise at 4 A.M. When they set out from Elmer's place in the old flatbed with the dogs, four in the front, two on Jack's lap, and 12 on the bed, it was still dark out, stars glowing above with the Milky Way still showing as a luminous band arcing the sky and the last of the moon dropping down behind them over the Sanders. They were off to mend some fence, the never-ending, always-there ranch chore. This section was stitched and stretched along a three-mile ragged line of weathered juniper posts that climbed and dipped among the native grasses, wiry sagebrush and prickly pear cactus. Elmer had not been over to this part of his land in years, but he seemed to remember that the last time when he was out "Chasing all hell and back after the damn grouse" that the barbed wire was rusting "pretty damn bad" and sagging "like my god-almighty-awful jowls." The drive to the work coursed along a red gravel road that turned into a dirt and rock two track. They crawled and bounced about a dozen miles up over bluffs, around enormous piles of eroding sandstone that looked like Egyptian monuments, and then a last run across a flat of "some of the finest damn grass in the West" according to Elmer. He'd purchased another 50 longhorns from a breeder up near Sweetgrass just south of the Alberta border and the cows were due in next week. He wanted them to fatten up and adjust to their new surroundings in this grass, but that old fence line needed to looking after. Elmer would never sell the cows. He was in love with the romanticism of having the Texas Longhorns roaming his land. He didn't need money, just an excuse to keep busy at this late stage of his life. Jack and Elmer would knock that work out today with steady, uninterrupted motion. Replace rotten posts with new steel ones. Pull up and tighten sagging strands of wire. Replace broken stretches and so on until the task was done. They'd worked together doing things like this hundreds of times over the years on both of their places. Fence lines, branding, neutering, haying, new barn roofs, all of the sweaty hard labor of their lives. Elmer had loaded up the truck with spools of wire, stakes, stretching equipment, coolers full of food, beer and plenty of water for all of them, including the dogs. Even in the dim light the temperature was already near seventy and appeared anxious to reach ninety by noon. As they approached a gate in the line, the day was fast turning from purpled dark to silver to yellow-gold seemingly all at once all across the east. Bands of blood red and pink-orange light flickered just above the horizon.

Elmer shut down the rig, the engine slowly coming to a stop in a series of pops, smoky belches and a final rattling, shimmying shiver that ended in the old engine wheezing into silence. Jack hopped out and headed for the gate where they'd pass through to run the line. The gate was a cobbled mess consisting of four strips of the wire attached to four grey juniper posts and hooked to a pole sunk into the ground. There were probably a million of these in this country, and Jack often thought he'd opened every damn one of them. He had the scars from the mean wire biting through his gloves to prove his point. Pulling on his gloves, he pushed on the fence for slack, pulled off the holding band and dragged the gate out of the way.

"Wire's not too bad, at least here, anyway. Those pine posts of years ago seem to be holding up okay, too," he said. "We'll kick this one in the ass by noon," and just as he was about to say some more a canine howl of enormous and now seemingly elliptical dimensions echoed across the lightening land, a sound so loud, so ancient even the breeze checked itself and died down into the rough grass. Addison and the rest of the dogs stopped dead. They'd been sniffing around a dried up antelope carcass over by the fence. Each dog sat down on its haunches and looked off to the east in the direction of a wind-carved bluff that looked something like the head of beaver, rounded head and slightly lower snout defined by eroded seams of sandstone and clinker. The sound came from over there.

The day grew lighter and hotter by the minute. The unearthly howl took forever to dissipate in the still air and when the cry was gone the land was without sound. Small birds ceased their chirping. Hawks and eagles were somewhere else now. A band of mule deer browsing a few hundred yards away when the men had first arrived were nowhere to be seen. Even the millions of grasshoppers were silent. It was like that ungodly howl had pierced the soul of this country and purged it of any pretensions to life.

Jack just stared until Elmer said, "A god-damned buffalo wolf or something even bigger and weirder, I'll bet my last pint of whiskey on it," and he pulled one from a pants pocket, took a deep swallow and lobbed it to Jack, who did the same. "Yeah, damn straight it's coming, all mad hell of it. Weather, fire, darkness. God only knows what the hell else," and Elmer never tells me what he really knows, the complete damn story. 'Let's get to this fence while before I expire from the stress of worrying about our little bit of the world."

The two men got down to it. The dogs remained motionless and silent until Addison stood and slowly walked to the top of a small rise and faced the bluff.

"*AAAHHRRGhhhh.*"

The dog listened as the sound returned softened and rearranged from bouncing around the rock and sand. Then it let loose again and again. The dog stared hard at the bluff, before finally sitting down to wait for as Elmer said, "God only knows what."

"Not in all my damned years, not in any single one of the full-tilt, crazy one of them, Jack. Not in all of them. Nothing like this god-blamed stuff of the past few weeks ever happened here. Damn near leaves me at a loss for words, and that ain't a good sign neither."

Jack finished crimping a strand of the biting wire, took off his heavy work gloves and looked up at Elmer, who was ratcheting a come-along to tighten the fence. He saw that the old man was not troubled or scared, but just plain amazed and mystified. He thought that Elmer had seen and done it all. The Workman proved him wrong.

They finished up the last section a little after noon. Most of the wire and posts would hold for a few more years, and didn't require their attention. Some of the stuff was rusted and broken. A few posts had weathered through. The hard part was sinking the steel post replacements down into three feet in the rock-hard ground. They worked a heavy, iron post pounder together, facing each other, grabbing the handles and banging the thing up and down on the tops of the post. The force of the effort slamming off the ground vibrated through their arms. The harsh metallic noise numbed their eardrums until all they heard was the ringing metal inside their heads.

Halfway through the line they came across a long-dead antelope that had died when it failed to clear the top strand of wire and tangled its hind feet. The poor beast's struggles to free itself had only made things worse. The wire was torn loose from the two nearest posts and wrapped tightly around the pronghorn's chest, cutting through the hide and digging into the rib bones. Neither man said a word as they clipped the strands of barbed wire and dragged the animal off into a clump of sage.

They ate a lunch of antelope steak sandwiches on rye bread, some of Elmer's homemade dill pickles. He used rye bread in the brine to ferment the cucumbers. The yeast did the job. And there was some potato salad spiked with jalapenos and Bermuda onions that Jack had put together the night before. A pair of huge Ponderosas provided shade from the sun, but little relief from the heat. They leaned back against the rough, red-rust bark and wound down from the work. The dogs were scattered about them lying on their sides, or on their stomachs with hind legs splayed backwards frog style. They'd consumed about ten pounds of dog chow and a few gallons of water. Snores, sleepy slobbering sounds, paws twitching in dreams, an ear flicking every now and then, that was it for the dog contingent. Addison, ever the avant-garde leader, was crashed out some feet from the others, belly basking in the sun, legs cast off at all angles, head lolling to one side, tongue hanging out almost into the grass.

"Damn dog's a piece of work," said Elmer as he worked on a can of cold beer. "Maybe I ought to enter that one in the Westminster Dog Show. Show those sissy-assed poodles a thing or two. Goddamn, you ever see those things when they show that piece of shit carnival on TV? Damn embarrassment to dogs the whole wide world. Awful. Just plain and simple awful.

"Now take my well-heeled pack here. They're all a bunch of loose-lipped idiots, but I love 'em just the same, especially now that they're little lame-brained insurrection's over. Hell, they were only acting on what was coming into their dog brains. Couldn't help themselves, the poor suckers." He started to say some more, but caught himself and instead pulled out another can of beer buried in the ice in a cooler he was using as an armrest. Elmer shook it up with a violent up and down motion, popped the tab and shot a spray at Addison, who only opened one eye, grunted and went back to sleep. "That wolf, the weather that's coming, Dark Star, the whole blasted bunch of it has those dogs sorely perplexed."

"Thanks for stopping before you got to the part about me and Natalie screwing on the side of the road. Don't know if I'll ever come to terms with all of it. Cuts through my guts. Makes me feel lost." Jack stopped, shook his head, then looked at Elmer. "How'd you know about all this bullshit with her?"

"Don't worry on that situation, Joseph. Time will take care of that. Hell, what's one more damned scar. Between us we got a shed full. Just keep pushing, grinding out the fucking days. You got no choice in the matter and you aren't the chickens hit suicide kind. Here," and he tossed a fresh pint of bourbon to Jack. "Works for me and I'm way too old to worry about those fools who think I've got a drinking problem. Hell yes I do. Had one all my life. Can't imagine life without whiskey or these genuine, made-in-Detroit cigars, either for that matter. Fuck 'em."

"Yeah, thanks for the sage wisdom, but answer my question. Did you know about her and me...and Foxen?" said Jack. "I never said a damn thing to you."

"Live long enough and you get pretty damn good at reading people and putting two and two together. It isn't brain surgery when you come moping around my place and head straight for the four-sided bottle. What else does that to a man? Missing a shot on a bird? A flat tire? Hell, I admit that the cheese has slipped off my cracker. That I'm a few bricks shy of a full load, and I don't have both oars in the water, either, but I can figure out a few things. I'm not that out of it."

"We're all out of it, Elmer," said Jack, but he was smiling a bit now. "Just crazy and senseless, but when I think on that, hell, when I think about it, maybe my life's been insane for a long time."

"Well, god-damn, the boy's finally figured this little out-of-tune ditty out. Course it's insane. The whole damn premise is built on our half-ass notions of what the world is. Crazy damn shit that is. But I know what you mean. I've been off my fine-tuned natural rhythm ever since I sold the mineral rights to Dark Star. Lost my edge. Can't even swear like an old rancher's supposed to anymore." He finished his beer and opened another. "Dark Star, you, me, we haven't done right by this country. Oh, we all got our lame-dick reasons and excuses. The country needs energy. I need the money. I care for the land. I've lived here all my life. What a load of horseshit. Tearing that coal out. My letting the bastards do it all the damned while kidding myself that it was a pissing joke and they'd never get away with any of it. Hell I don't need the money. I got more than I'll ever need." He paused to light the stub of cigar wedged in a corner of his mouth. "That dead antelope. My fence killed it. Nothing else. Who in the Sam hell am I kidding? Not the land. It knows better. I can't explain this to you buddy, but the land knows, more than us and we feel it, but damn well choose to ignore the truth. The dogs really feel it. And that huge, big ass wolf is here to make sure we get the point."

Jack bummed one of Elmer's green cigars and torched the tip, inhaled the smoke, then blew the grey-blue stuff out through his lips and nose.

"No one's ever seen that wolf, Elmer. Probably just the way the wind works through the rock."

Elmer stared hard at his friend.

"Just when I start to think that your half-assed pea brain may actually hold a thought or two, you prove me dead wrong, Jack. Damn, face the truth out here. At least some of it before you die an ignorant fool. We all think we're so fucking smart. So hip, to use one of those crazy jazz horn blowers of yours terms. Horrible music. Simply horrible. Sounds like someone's strangling a rabid otter. God almighty. Art my ass."

A puff on the cigar and a swig of beer.

"We don't know diddly about the natural world, about what we call home or our land. Not shit for Shinola. If we could ever drop our lame-ass egos and admit that we're plain, shit-for-brains stupid, we'd know a hell of a lot more, but enough of this crap. I brought my Winchester pump. Barrels dirty some but it shoots and I tossed in the Wingmaster for you. Let's see if these worthless pieces of canine shit can hunt. Shells and guns are in the tool chest. Help an old man out. I got another beer and another sip of this real, high class whiskey to attend to,"

"Damn, Elmer, you surprise the hell out of me sometimes."

"Don't start with that shit now. I'm no genius, but I'm vaguely aware of some of the insane bullshit that goes on around here. Lord damn Christ. The boy thinks I'm an idiot. You dogs hear that? Well, get off your dead butts and lets roust some birds. About eight or ten would be real good burned all to hell on the grill the way that man over there does it. Fucking pyromaniac to my way of thinking. Come on. Up all of you mongrel jokes. Get up."

Elmer was standing now, reaching for the shotgun Jack was handing him. All sixteen Boykins were up and circling like mad around the two men. Hopping in the air and creating a mad din filled with barks, excited coughs, and moans. Sixteen tails wagging like crazy. Addison was whining, groaning and laughing all at once, sparks flying from those amber eyes. The game was afoot and all of them were ready.

"Prettiest damn noise on earth. Lot better than that jazz shit of yours. Hampton Hawes. Miles Davis. Horace Silver. Lord save my ragged soul. Who the hell are these people? Give me these slap happy dogs wailing away out here any day."

The air was really hot now. Finding birds on a blue-sky afternoon like this one would be tough. They hiked over a ridge and dropped down into a brushy draw that held the dying remains of a small spring and some shade. A few striped tree frogs croaked away as they approached, but the sound stopped when the dogs began working the bushes. Midges and electric-blue damsel flies buzzed above small pockets of still water puddled up in depressions in the rock streambed. Leeches and small larva wriggled through the bright green scum on the edges of this water. The dogs scoured the cover, routing under clumps of juniper, nosing through the grass, around brushy piles of rock, everywhere. They were intent on their task, looking back every now and then to see where the two men were, sometimes waiting on them to catch up.

They walked down the drainage without the dogs turning birdy once. The place seemed lifeless from a grouse standpoint. The wind flowed through the tops of the old pines making a soft, lonely sigh. They walked across a grass and sage flat to another draw that opened where a large stand of Ponderosa began. No water showing here. Just a few moist spots in the dark, grassy, shaded reaches.

"We'll push up this mother, then work across the flat above," said Elmer. "Always some sharps on top crunching the crickets. We'll get our supper."

This draw was more of the first. A few insects, scattered patches of shade and lots of heat. Jack was sweating when they broke loose out on the open flat.

The afternoon breeze ran warm but cooled him all the same. He looked over at Elmer. The old guy was dry as a bone and breathing normally, like he'd been sitting in his porch rocker for the past two hours.

They stopped for a short break, a snack and, most importantly, to water the dogs. Elmer pulled a two-gallon jug from his canvas rucksack, kneeled down and poured the water in a bowl he'd brought for this purpose. The Boykins lined up in single file led by their fearless leader Addison and drank their fill. He drained the one jug and pulled out another.

"Polite bunch of miscreant farts, aren't they. Yeah, you're all a bunch of good ones, and I forgive you the past weeks' foolishness. Good dogs. Let's hunt up some grouse so we can watch our friend here put on one of his famous shooting displays. Keep your tails low, he's a ground sluicer at heart."

Elmer looked over at Jack and laughed, a sound a lot like his dogs' bark.

"Glad to be rid of the water. Thirty damn pounds weighs hard on an old man's back. Crickets are here, so are the birds. Be alert."

The crickets were everywhere. Crawling and hopping at Jack's feet. Big black ones the size of figs. They began to work through the knee-high, golden dry grass, the dogs swinging back and forth about twenty yards in front of them.

Then Addison stopped dead, like someone had frozen the spaniel in time. The dog's body was stretched like an arrow pointing at a large clump of sage and dense grass. Front right paw curled up, tail straight and slightly angled to the sky. The other dogs went motionless, honoring their leader's point.

"Get ready. She's gonna bust loose any second."

The two men moved forward slowly, walking like the ground was littered with eggshells, shot guns in the ready position. Then, sounding like a helicopter gone mad, a half dozen sage grouse, big ones, seven or eight pounds each, whomped up out of the sage, wings beating frantically. Squawking and clucking in alarm as only the big grouse can. As soon as they got up above the cover they cut with the breeze and began to sail away. Elmer dropped one on a swinging shot to the left and another as it raced downwind. Both birds crumpled then smacked into the ground, feathers everywhere. Jack missed one in front of him, then nailed another about forty yards out. All of this seemed like it was happening at once – brown, tan, grey feathers and beating wings, gunfire, smoke, leaping and barking dogs, tufts of brown fur flying everywhere. The dogs broke off into three groups and ran down the birds. As always. Addison was in the lead and went after Jack's kills. When the Boykin tried to retrieve the Sage hen, the bird turned out to be quite alive though one wing was broken. The grouse stood its ground then leaped at the dog who in turn hopped straight up off the ground and pounced on the bird, snapping its neck in one swipe of its jaws.

"Damn sure as hell wouldn't want that one mad at me," said Elmer. His faced was flushed with the thrill of shooting and the rush of killing. Jack was the same. "God damn I love this shit," said Elmer. Then he let out a deep bass howl that carried far across the Workman. The dogs looked at their leader and did the same. The land vibrated with the energy. All here was as it should be again. Wild, alive, filled with untamed insanity.

"Christ, beat-it-all-to-hell. Now we're living. Damn sage hens aren't the best eating, but I'm sure you'll find a work-around on that one. Thought we'd scare up the sharps. Didn't figure on the Sage hens being here for a few more weeks yet. Here, take a pull on this and have one of these fine cigars."

"When I'm done with those birds, they'll taste damn good, Elmer. Count on it."

The dogs were in a semi-circle around the two, a pair of sage hens dropped on the ground between them. Addison pushed through the pack, dragging a bird that must have weighed in at ten pounds. She released the grouse right on top of Elmer's boots, looked up and barked a little tune that seemed to say "We're in tall grass now, boss." Elmer bent over and rubbed her ears.

"Fine work there, buddy. Goes for the rest of you crazy hounds, too. Damn fine dog work. You done your breed proud and warmed an old, crazy bastard's heart. Yeah we're in tall grass and were living damn large this here moment."

The two men lit up, the cheap cigars, now quite dry from the day's heat and nonexistent humidity, torching in a cloud of smoke. They worked on the whiskey and cans of warm beer, shared an honest smile of old friends and just plain laughed out loud. "Life is good Jack. Tough as a hell. A mean son-of-a-bitch, but don't this beat all? Real hunting dogs. World class cigars. Smooth whiskey and all of this."

Elmer held his shotgun out away from him and swung it back and forth to take in The Workman shining and blasting away all around them.

~ ~ ~

He was on his hands and knees hiding behind a small clump of willows, peering into the water while dozens of his brown trout gorged on caddisfly nymphs as the little things wriggled their way up to the surface to emerge as fluttering, gray helicopters. The brown trout flashed copper and bronze as they twisted and turned this way and that chasing the caddis. He could see the white of their mouths as they opened and closed. And he could see their crimson and black spots as the fish twisted their bodies to snare the food. One brown in particular caught his attention. A trophy by this stream's standards. Eleven, twelve inches. The fish held on the bottom near the far bank as a small slip of current pushed the nymphs directly to him. Only minor flickings of its tail and fins were necessary to hold position as the brown sucked in the insects. Suddenly from beneath an undercut grassy bank a few feet downstream from the big brown a fat, bright-orange submarine emerged, ponderously working its way upstream. He stared through the water as the twenty-inch fish nosed among the streambed cobble kicking up the nymphs with little bursts of sand. The creature appeared to be a giant goldfish. 'A Koi," he thought as he picked up his bamboo rod and dropped a short cast several feet in front of the behemoth. 'Must have washed through the dam from the reservoir and found its way through Dark Star's sludge and up my creek,' he figured. 'Crazy Drew locals drop damn near anything in there. Goldfish, muskies, salmon, probably even jellyfish. Who the hell knows what all?' His weighted Hare's ear nymph, a pattern of tan feathers and fur, sank to the bottom right in line with the course of the Koi. He twitched the fly with a slight tug on his line and the fish surged up to it and took. He drove the hook's barb home by sharply lifting up the rod, and hung on as the intruder surged all over the small pool scattering terrified brown trout in every direction. The trout fled in a flurry of miniature wakes and sparkling splashes. The Koi must have weighed close to three pounds and the lightweight fly rod was bent in an exaggerated U-shape. Back and forth the fish went pulling powerfully. He hoped his slender leader would hold and that his fine rod would not splinter under the strain. The tug-of-war went on for twenty minutes. The bottom of the pool was cloudy from the fine sand stirred up by the Koi. He stood next to the bank now. The fish swam in small circles and listed to one side. He pulled the fish to him and to the surface. The Koi was exhausted, gills flapping open and closed. It rolled over on its belly and he bent down and snatched it by the tail, lifting it far above his trout stream in a spray of water. The iridescent oranges and yellows of the Koi glistened in the sun. A glowing presence that somehow had found its way from someone's aquarium all the way up to the Workman Plateau. Quite a journey. A beautiful fish.

"Where did you come from," he asked as he moved his head right up to the Koi's, whose thick, rubbery lips puckered and unpuckered. The eyes of the fish seemed to look through him without any hint of awareness or comprehension of the difficult spot it was now in hanging upside down in the hot breeze and several feet from the safety of the cool water burbling beneath its head. "Maybe from Paris, Texas" and he laughed. "I hope not."

He got down on his knees and placed the Koi back in the stream. The brown trout scattered at this intrusion into their cold, clear world, but soon they returned and watched from a distance, their bodies quivering with fear and curiosity. He moved the fish slowly side to side in the current. The well-oxygenated water slowly brought it back to life and with a pulse of its tail the Koi swam free. He watched as the orange fish resumed feeding on the caddis nymphs.

"Where did you come from?" he asked again. "Where does any of this come from?"

He stood there for hours staring at his brown trout as they fed, now on the surface as another, larger species of caddis began whirring and swooping above and across the water. The Koi disappeared from view somewhere around the bend. The browns just kept sipping the bugs. The late summer air was dry, but the stream smelled rich, full of life, almost sensual. The sun set in a blaze of orange and a mantle of purple. As it grew dark the stars came out.

He never moved. Jack was linked to the moving water and the feeding fish. To all of it.

~ ~ ~

The motel where they spent time together was located along the old highway west of the Interstate a few miles south of Drew. Foxen was a bold man but he was also discreet. No rendezvous at the hotel on Main. Drew was a small town trying to grow itself big, but it was provincial small and that meant that everyone pretty much knew everyone and everyone's business – who was drinking too much, who was broke, who was beating who and, number one on the list, who was screwing who. Well, Foxen, for largely subconscious reasons, had been screwing the Graves clan for decades, and wanted to keep at it. And he didn't need a bunch of northern high plains idiots up in arms and banded against him for violating some lame code of the west or whatever. All dark work benefited from stealth. He'd screwed Jack's father out of his land and coal, Jack out of his land, water, coal and way of life, and out of what Jack liked to think of as his woman. Natalie. Yeah, dear sweet, sexy and hard as nails Natalie. Foxen had tumbled on to her during a preliminary meeting concerning mining the coal buried beneath the Workman Plateau. That was a few years back over at the Dark Star McCoy offices. A meeting of geologists, hydrologists, biologists (hence Natalie) and a few attorneys thrown into the mix to make a thoroughly roguish gathering. She did her bit there filling in the others on the curious ways of water in a parched land and its impact on the country. Now you see it and now you don't. Underground rivers and aquifers resembling subterranean lakes moved as if by magic through the porous layers of sandstone, limestone and the rambling cracks between beds of clinker, shale and, of course, coal. To count on tapping this water to put out what she termed even at this early stage 'fires from hell,' water to douse the burning seams of coal at Yoter's and other locations on the plateau, to count on this water would be foolish, she said. And using this water may dry up the small creeks and springs on the plateau creating havoc and devastation for both the flora and fauna up there. Other geologists and hydrologists slouched around the table ridiculed her assessments and opinions, saying that there was more than enough water to put out a thousand fires, and that the land would be fine regardless of the final state of the aquifer. There was plenty of water. Enough to last for centuries. Natalie stuck to her guns and closed with a vehement "The bunch of you are not only assholes, you're also inbred, subnormal morons," and then she flashed each of the men and the one other woman in the room the most charming, subtly blatant, sexual smile Foxen had ever seen. After the meeting he called her aside and asked her to dinner and drinks. She accepted. She had always been drawn to older men. That dinner led to the first night at the motel south of town. The one with the hot pink and green neon trim that lit the eves and flashed over and over Rockin R Motel. The one with the black-and-white TVs, no phones, and off-white chintz bedspreads. That was the first of many nights over the years, the frequency actually increasing after she started hanging around with Jack. Foxen and Natalie had what each other wanted. She liked screwing her surrogate father – the all too common Elektra Complex in full regalia. He liked the idea of screwing the daughter he never had. And with her ongoing relationships with both Foxen and Jack, Natalie was in a constant state of intense sexual arousal. She glowed and burned like the coal on

Elmer's land. Foxen knew about Jack, and he anticipated the day when he could stick it to the "half-assed" still another time, this time with the out front, blatant knowledge that he was fucking the guy's woman. Why Foxen hated Graves even he didn't know. He'd thought on this, often and all of it came back to the fact that he only knew that he wanted them to suffer and to see their lives destroyed. To feel otherwise would have meant casting his whole life, his reason for being, into doubt. Doubt was something Foxen never entertained. So he had flown up from Denver the next day like he told Kilduff he would. And he made it clear to Kilduff that nothing was going to stop Dark Star from getting the coal underneath the Workman and Yoter's place in particular. The conglomerate never backed down. Money wasn't the issue. Power and the exercising of that power was what all of this was about. Never show weakness or capitulation. Never. And the two men drank whiskey and smoked cigars to seal that fate. Foxen was intoxicated from wielding his power, and Kilduff, against his best judgment, yielded. He had to choose between preserving his life or his job. He chose his job. So Foxen screwed Natalie. Natalie screwed Jack. And Jack, Elmer and the dogs howled at the moon.

"Jack knows about us," she said.

"Fuck him," he said.

~ ~ ~

The next morning Natalie pulled her pickup alongside an island at a gas station-mini- market in Drew and got out, as did her companion, Foxen. He pushed the appropriate button on one of the pumps, slid his credit card through the slot and pushed more buttons before the machine said 'Begin pumping fuel,' which she did. Unleaded Supreme. Foxen went inside to grab a couple of packs of Newports for her. While the thirty-gallon tank swallowed the over-priced fuel, a steady, though tiny, stream of the stuff leaked onto the concrete. A hole the size of a twenty-penny nail had been poked through the pipe leading to the tank, perhaps from a strand of barbwire or perhaps from a twenty-penny nail kicked up by the truck's tires while Natalie wheeled along the Workman's back roads. By the time Foxen returned she was putting the nozzle back in place at the pump. Neither of them noticed the puddle of gas beneath the truck. The station always smelled of gasoline, so nothing seemed unusual.

They both turned from looking at each other just as Jack drove up to another island of pumps some sixty feet away. He jumped out of the truck, pressed the 'Pay cash inside button,' and began fueling his rig. He looked up just as Foxen returned to Natalie's truck. He had seen Jack. Jack had seen him. Foxen put his arm around Natalie. She looked up at him and smiled. Then she saw Jack.

Foxen turned her head to face him and gave her a long kiss. She made a weak attempt to pull away as she glanced at Jack, an expression of fear and confusion distorting her features.

Jack was at his limit with all of it – the haul road, the loss of his land because of the coal his father had sold, Natalie, Foxen – all of it. He looked at the .357 lying on the truck's bench seat, finished filling up the truck, replaced the hose and went for his gun. He came around the back of his old truck with the pistol held slightly above waist level, just in time to see Foxen puffing on a cigar and lighting a smoke for Natalie with an Ohio Blue Tip stick match. The two of them exhaled and laughed at him, cruel, ugly expressions leering through their tobacco smoke – Natalie high with her confused rage and her desire to control Jack. Foxen buzzing from the hate that ruled his existence. Jack took aim at Natalie. Foxen, unaware of the pistol pointed at her, casually tossed the still flaming match with a flick of his fingers. It curved, still burning, towards the ground where it would land in the pool of gas.

He leveled the gun's bead on her head and her eyes went wide with fear. He prepared to squeeze the trigger, taking time to consider whether he really wanted to kill someone he loved and who he thought had loved him. He hated her, too and seeing her with Foxen was hellish and ripped at his insides. He wanted them both dead. Out of his life. Never to have existed. And he still loved her and knew he couldn't kill her. Killing Foxen meant nothing to him. Dead or alive this man was just one more shitty human to Jack. The world was full of them. And Natalie, she was love to him and more pain in his life. Someone who gave a little of herself when it suited her purposes or satisfied her needs. He always fell for this, believing the little was the beginning of much more. It never was. The giving was nothing more than taking and he was tired of all of it. Alone was better. He could count on that. He thought this just as the gas ignited with a "whomp" ripping away the pipe to the gas tank and setting off the fuel inside. Thirty gallons of high-octane gasoline ignited in a yellow-gold explosive roar that blew the rear end of the truck up and then the whole thing slowly turned over on its side. What he saw was Natalie's mouth saying 'No. Please don't, Jack' and her body starting to slump toward the ground. Maybe from stress. Maybe she was fainting. Then she was shoved forward by the blast and simultaneously enveloped in burning gasoline. The explosion had slammed Jack against the tailgate and knocked him to the pavement. He heard her scream 'Oh God! Jack help me.' Not Foxen's name, but his, and he knew then despite all of her meanness and selfishness that he had touched her somewhere inside and that in her own way, she loved him, too. Her hair blazed skyward in a flaming headdress. Foxen had time to form an embryonic look of stunned terror before he, too, was engulfed in flames. Jack watched as the burning body lurched to him in hideous, staggering steps then collapsed. Screams of agony, of pure intense pain, reached him. He could already smell the cooked flesh mixed with the odors of burning paint, tires and fuel. The hair on his arms and head was singed, as was his shirt. His skin felt like it had been burned.

All of this took place in seconds, but already he thought he could hear the wails of police, fire, and ambulance sirens. Natalie and Jack's trucks had been the only vehicles at the station. He turned to his left and saw the attendant staring through a shattered window, the phone still held to his ear. Displays of cigarettes, lighters and candy had been knocked all over the counter from the concussion of the blast. The kid's mouth hung open. Looking back he saw a blackened form that was Natalie. Foxen's body was also charred black and bubbly, smoldering with more smoke than flame now. Her truck was burning steadily, especially the tires that were billowing a thick, blue-black, greasy smoke.

Jack turned to the street and spotted two bright red fire trucks, lights flashing, pulling up to the simmering wreckage. A pair of white-and-orange ambulances were right behind as was Egyptian Healy in his cruiser followed by a Wyoming state patrol car. 'Probably my twisted buddy from Paris, Texas,' he thought. The scene was now filled with the deafening screams of sirens and strobing flashes of red, blue, white and yellow flashing lights. He crawled to the cab of his truck and shoved the .357 under the seat amid a mess of crushed beer cans, brake fluid containers, wrenches and lots of dirt and mud-caked weeds. He saw blood running down his cheeks and chin and soaking his shirt. He could feel something warm and sticky draining from his ears. Then he passed out, his head knocking against the rusty running board.

~ ~ ~

Rough weather on the Workman. Nothing new. Wild storm fronts steaming up from the Gulf of Mexico, surging in from the Pacific or wailing down from Alberta bringing severe wind, insane lightning, white-out blizzards, cloudbursts, hail, sleet, intense heat, and numbing cold year after year. Two feet of snow in May. Thunderstorms in January. One-hundred-twenty degrees in July. Minus forty in March. Or plus sixty in February. None of this is uncommon on the Workman Plateau. The jet stream tracks directly across this country or oscillates just to the north or south of here.

Rough weather can look like a drought. The last week of September brought with it cloudless skies and temperatures in the mid-nineties. Record highs. The land was cooked to a dry withered, golden brown. The softening light of autumn shone and flickered through the tall, dead grasses and now-silvery sage with an unearthly intensity that flickered and played across the wind-polished surfaces of grass stems and seed heads, the radiance turning on and off, expanding and contracting at the whim of the warm breeze. In the mornings the light dew glistened in the orange light of sunrise and looked like fields of highly-polished diamonds, rubies, emeralds and sapphires that had sprouted atop slender stalks of crystal, a vision offering prismatic magic that was at once spectacular to behold and blinding in its short-lived brilliance. But by midday the indigo sky was cooked to a sun-blasted white, the intensity of the noon light washed out the landscape, everything out here. Ponderosas, yucca, sage, buffalo grass, all of it looked like it was part of an over-exposed photograph. The red, orange, ochre, lavender and brown soils of the plateau held no moisture. The two-track and dirt roads that wound across and up and down the Workman, rising up through now bone dry coulees, up through parched stands of willow, alder and large cottonwoods with their thick, rough gray bark and then finally they drifted across the swales and flats of the plateau, those roads were covered with two, three, four inches of powdery soil that streamed behind a rancher's pickup like a wake behind a ship at sea. Devil winds whizzed and spun through the country, the whirling funnels now red, now brown, now shades of yellow, now a mixture of the all of the soils' colors.

The entire Workman appeared lifeless in this first week of fall. Antelope, mule deer, turkeys, hawks, rabbits, snakes, even the spiders and ants, along with almost every other creature living here was either underground or hunkered down beneath the brush or overhanging rock outcroppings near dwindling springs. Cattle were dropping from thirst and hunger by the dozens everywhere, their pitiful bellowings rising hoarsely up from ponds that were now nothing more than cracked mud holes. The animals crowded together and pawed in vain the hard ground. Angus and Hereford carcasses lay on their sides in the coulees and on the flats where the animals had looked for water, the desiccated hides stretched tight to ripping across thick ribs. Turkey vultures feasted and were the only ones who thrived in the blistering drought. Creeks were dried up, gone, nothing but dust-covered rocks and floury silt. Needles on the Ponderosa were more gray than green. The layers of multi-colored rock that made up the bluffs, buttes and cliffs of the land, the exposed black seams of coal, the yellow, charcoal and celadon thrustings of sandstone, the orange-brown chunks of clinker, all of this rock and soil stood out in the heat beneath the dead sky in muted colors. The bizarrely eroded escarpments and pillars of stone looked like they had been lightly covered with white spray paint.

Spontaneous combustion wildfires burned thousands of acres of the grassy flats and stands of pine, the fires only giving it up when they came to stretches of land that was nothing more now than dirt and rock. The air was often bitter with smoke until a hot afternoon wind blew the acrid stuff off toward South Dakota to the east. Then the air smelled only of the hot sun and the overwhelming dryness. The seams of burning coal kept simmering, turning a hot landscape into a surreal furnace. Mirages from the heat made the land look as though it was being viewed through cataracts as the country wavered and distorted in the baking air.

The Workman appeared dead for now. Life had turned invisible. Rain and snow would bring the country back next year, but this season was over, finished.

Precipitation was overdue and desperately needed to nourish the roots of all the plants that grew here, and the game was dying of a desperate thirst.

Would the wet weather ever come ranchers asked her over drinks in local bars? Would it ever come before the Workman was completely and absolutely reduced to ash and cinders?

In the long-term scheme of things these were foolish questions. Of course the storms would come with their billions of tons of moisture. Cactus, sage, Ponderosa, coyote, mule deer, they'd all hang in there, more than likely in diminished numbers but they'd come back when the Workman flowed again. The rain-laden clouds always returned and as a matter of fact a huge storm was building now, the kind that only hits the Workman Plateau maybe every thousand years or so, a storm that would wash away the drought and a good deal more.

An enormous mass of warm, moist air was pulsing up from the Gulf. Uncommon but not unheard of for this time of year. And a Pacific system was slowly spinning like a miniature galaxy in the direction of the Sanders Mountains, the thick clouds riding in from the coast across Oregon and Washington. Lenticular clouds, curving brush strokes of moisture, were already arcing over the peaks of the Sanders, a sure sign of the harsh weather soon to come. To the north a dense mass of cold air was sweeping down from the arctic gathering still more moisture as it raced along the east slope of the Canadian Rockies. The eternal high pressure that had been locked over the Workman for weeks, the high that had been punishing the country for what seemed like forever to those who lived here, was about to be shoved east.

A storm was coming, but for now the land was lifeless and baking in the heat.

~ ~ ~

Around noon several days after the explosion at the gas station Jack and Elmer were sitting on the hood of Elmer's truck sharing a bottle of Jim Beam Rye, a semi-serious, whiskey change-of-pace that brought a smile to the old man's suntanned and wind-burned face.

It was another hot day, but finally after many weeks there were clouds building over the Sanders Mountains and all along the western horizon. Perhaps some moisture was in sight.

"Haven't had a bottle of this shit in years," said Elmer as he took a decent hit. "Damn good booze, though," and he wiped his mouth on his shirtsleeve. "Whiskey, rye whiskey. Whiskey I cry. If I don't get rye whiskey. I surely must die. Yes indeed. Nothing like it."

"It goes down. That's all I ask," and Jack winked at Elmer who smiled in the recognition that his friend was healing up, coming back from his private hell of the past few months. "Haven't had any either in a bit. Not since I brought you that case when you helped me with the calving in '93." Jack lit a Camel, took a drink from the bottle and set it on the hood. "That was a bitch of a spring, Elmer. Snowed all of March, most of April and then some more in May."

"Like that sometimes," said Elmer as he flicked pieces of bacon rind to the Boykins seated in their usual semi-circle around the two men. He'd fried up several pounds of the tough meat the other day, the pork a gift from Coaker, who'd butchered a pair of his Landrace hogs. Tenderloins and two-inch-thick pork chops were also part of the package. Elmer would reciprocate the next time he cut up one of his Angus. He did have a couple of dozen Texas Longhorns fattening up on some fenced acreage along some bottom land by the Dolphy River, but he could never bring himself to kill them, always saying that every time he looked at "their scrawny asses and long-beat-all-to-hell'-pointed horns," he started feeling "all romantic with it all." When Jack heard that, he gave Elmer a good deal of static along lines of "Montana is where men are men and sheep are scared," modified with the longhorn variation. Elmer would just laugh it away and say that he'd gotten all he wanted when he was younger, and Jack would counter with "Sheep or steers?" and then Elmer would laugh again and say, "You're a twisted shit, Jack old boy."

The two had been discussing the aftermath of the explosion at the gas station. The paramedics had taken

Jack to the Drew hospital where he'd spent a couple of days with a concussion and some secondary burns along his arms and face. IVs, hospital food and officious nurses drove him out of the place as soon as he was able to sit up and locate his clothes, at least what was left of them. Shirt and T-shirt had been delicately pulled from his burns and then discarded, so Jack checked himself out wearing jeans, boots and a hospital gown. "Worn worse," he said to the nurse. After that he'd killed the ensuing weeks drinking more than usual, which meant a lot, fixing fence, coping with his cattle and dealing with Natalie's death. Her remains had been sent back to Wisconsin to be buried next to the rest of her family at a small cemetery along Turtle Creek in the southern part of the state. The lack of a funeral and a wake to grieve her loss hadn't helped Jack any. He'd spoken with Elmer some about how he felt and his friend would smile ruefully and say, "Stay with it. All you can do is keep pushing. Pain always goes away, at least enough so you can get on with whatever this damned life has for us poor bastards next." Jack would return home and sit next to his little spring-fed trout stream, burning up the hours watching the brown trout as they fed on the emerging caddis and even some small stoneflies that buzzed near the water's surface and among the willows. The fish never stopped feeding. 'Do they ever rest?' he wondered. 'God! I'd sure like to. I'm beat.' He'd be up at all hours of the night brooding about his life and seeing nothing good in it. And he'd listen to a life-hardened band called Wilco, music Elmer actually liked as opposed to Coltrane. "Jazz. Shit. Sounds like someone pulling the tail off one of my dogs with vice grips. That's nothin' but pure as shit simple noise, son. Listen to Hank or Conway or Ferlon. Now that's some serious damn music. Those boys could carry a tune, but these guys ain't bad" Jack would shrug and even smile at this and say "The song Bull Black Nova" makes sense to me'"

Blood in the sink, blood in the trunk. High at the wheel of a bull black Nova And I'm sorry as a setting sun. This can't be undone, can't be outrun

Elmer would say "now there's some words I can sink my teeth into," and smile at Jack." And later on in the dark sitting outside under an eternity of stars and galaxies with the help Coltrane's rhythms he'd always make it through the interminable night and by sunrise he'd be ready to face another day, eventually even with a trace of optimism.

After a couple of weeks he had put the memory of Natalie in a place where it didn't dominate his life. He was at the stage where he could go about the day-to-day routine without thinking of her constantly. When he did remember her now, it felt like he was thumbing through an old photo album. Memories, some painful, some happy, but nothing that sliced through him like a jagged knife blade. That part of it was mostly over, but for some time after her death, usually around 3 A.M., Jack would roll out of his sweat-soaked bed, pull on jeans and a shirt and go to the kitchen where he'd build a fire in the wood stove and turn on Coltrane and his tenor sax before starting in on the whiskey, chain smoking his Camels and calling up the image of her in his mind and the memories of all that had passed between them.

"Fucking Foxen," he'd say.

"Fucking women," he'd say.

He'd loved her, still did way down deep in his heart and gut, but her sleeping with that bastard, a man who'd taken advantage of him and his father for decades, that thought, that horrible image would never go away and it would always darken his thoughts of her. He hated her. He always would. And he loved her. He always would. He was tired and sick of all of the pain that had shaped his life. He just wanted to live, to be left alone with some semblance of peace. "Run out the goddamned string," he'd mutter. And he'd say after he was very drunk, hand raised towards the eternal night sky out there above the kitchen ceiling, hand raised, middle finger extended, he'd say "The hell with you, God. The hell with you," and he'd think with a grim smile sliding across his face, "The hell with hell. I'm already there." Then he'd see her face and bare breasts leaning over him as he came-to the day they'd found the bison skull and he'd hurt like the hell he was living in and he'd say,

"Fucking women."

But even this misery was fading from his life. The sun kept burning up over the eastern edge of the plateau each morning and he did keep going, finding pleasure in the hard work of ranching. His dreams were gone up in smoke. Like Natalie and Foxen he'd think and then say, "God! Elmer's right. I really am a twisted bastard," and he'd go back to his fencing. All he wanted now was to slide through the days without any additional pain. He'd really had enough. The whiskey helped some, but not much and he began to ease off the stuff. Instead, when the bottle beckoned he'd walk the ravines and sage flats with his old banged up Remington 870 Wingmaster, a gun his father had given him when he was eleven. He'd dropped a lot of birds with the gun. Sage grouse, sharptails, huns, chukar, pheasants, even turkeys. Despite the brutal weather there were plenty of birds this year and Jack had little trouble kicking up bunches of sharps as he pushed up brushy draws. Twenty, thirty, forty of the birds would explode from the brush in a whirring, clucking dusky-colored cloud of beating wings. And he raise the gun to his shoulder automatically swinging through one of the grouse, both eyes open, pull the trigger and then swing on another and shoot again. He did this so quickly, he often had time to see both birds tumble into the dry grass in soft heaps and he'd watch as tufts of feathers drifted down through the lifeless air. Then he'd walk up the rest of the now scattered grouse and shoot some more. He'd do this every afternoon right when the sun began dropping down to the western mountains. He'd walk and flush the sharptails and shoot a half-dozen or so and then he'd wander the flats working up a six or seven-pound sage hen or two. He'd get on them quickly, before they had time to work their wings to maximum thrust and power away from him in seconds. Most people didn't like the strong, gamy taste of these birds, but he did. He'd soak them in milk for hours, rinse them, then marinade them in a mixture of white wine, olive oil, bay leaf, rosemary, lots of garlic, salt, freshly ground pepper and a bunch of sliced lemons. Then he'd grill them over a hot fire, constantly basting the browning flesh with the marinade. A green salad and the grouse, some sharpies, too, and maybe a bottle of the Merlot, and then he'd go out on the porch and sip some whiskey and smoke his Camels well into the dark, star-packed night. That's how he lived now. Ranch work. Shooting birds. Drinking some, smoking, watching his brown trout and thinking, and sometimes talking with Elmer. He was finding out about inner quiet and peace for the first time in his life and the stillness within him was at once frightening, lonely and powerful. The strength and serenity of isolation and calmness were making his life bearable and moving him further in distant directions, territory where he was completely alone with his thoughts but at the same time completely aware of others wandering the same wavelengths. Voices would come to his internal conversations and talk with him like old friends do around a nighttime fire with a shared bottle. All of them sounding different but all of them familiar in unremembered ways. Like seeing a river somewhere for the first time and recognizing that the riffles, pools and brushy banks were a lot like his miniature trout stream. The voices were like that. Nothing outrageously revelatory. Just talk in his head with those he'd never met, but had always known. "You're completely nuts, buddy," he'd say out loud and he'd laugh and the voices would say 'We all are. Who cares?' And he grew used to his new way of hearing things and he never said a word about this to Elmer, but one night the old guy looked at him with a glint in his eyes and said "Crazy as all hell are the voices we listen to, but it beats the good goddamned hell out of pretending we don't hear them, don't it Jack," and before he could reply, Elmer was off by the back porch feeding the sixteen Boykins, and Jack just looked at all of them and up at the sky and inside himself and said softly "Damn right, Elmer."

After Foxen was killed his remains were shipped back to Denver in a company jet, cremated, a redundant touch Jack thought, and buried in some cemetery near Arvada. He'd purchased a plot there amid the condos and high rises that had once been sage hills and flats. Kilduff convinced the Dark Star board to pull off of the Workman and stick with the McCoy mine, work that land over until it played out in another ten or fifteen years. Then the Consortium would move on to another part of the planet and start all over with the scraping, blasting and digging. For now, at least, the Workman Plateau was spared and so was Jack's place. The haul road was still in, but Dark Star had graded it over and scattered some wild grass seed over the dirt, the thin kernels lying on the soil baking under the sun or blowing away in the dust with the onset of the predictable hot afternoon wind. The water pumping gear had been hauled away a few weeks back. Huge trucks carried the skeleton-like drilling structure, the large pumping equipment and all of the piping back to McCoy. As for the new rail line, that was on hold. The one already at Decker could handle that mine's coal output. The river had been spared, too, for a few years, anyway. It was already washing away much of the damage done by the construction. Oil-covered gravel and soaked soil were sucked up by the patient river's current and carried downstream towards the Yellowstone River more than a hundred miles to the north. Maybe the material would eventually find its way to the Gulf of Mexico. At least St. Louis. The environmentalists proclaimed Dark Star's pullout on the Workman as a "blow for the earth and our environmental crusade." So they went off to fight their holy war somewhere else. Something about slaughtered bison or maybe it was the grizzlies up along the Swan Crest in northwestern Montana.

For the first few weeks after the explosion the conversation in Drew and among area ranchers was dominated by the fiery deaths of Natalie and Foxen, and the fact that the disaster took place right in front of Jack's eyes, that part, right in front of his eyes, was a big selling point. The horror of watching other humans burn to death in unimaginable agony worked its perverse magic on the people's minds for many hours and across the distorted insights of countless drinks. But like people everywhere, after pounding the subject matter over from all angles at least ten thousand times, the story grew old, especially when news broke that Wyoming's governor had been discovered by his wife's private investigator alone in a Cheyenne motel room with two fourteen year-old boys. That one would play for a month or so anyway. Perversion in its varied forms always pulled at people's minds. "Never get enough of that shit," Elmer said.

Life went on all along the Workman. Jack's physical wounds healed with some scarring. His emotional injuries knitted, also, but with some scar tissue of their own and life did indeed roll on. And Jack found himself at Elmer's this morning with the rye whiskey and he even felt happy for the first time in many long weeks. Elmer noticed the change in attitude. He clapped him on the shoulder and said "Not bad half-ass shape for a spineless dipshit like yourself. Beginnin' to think you're gonna make it. God help us all." Then he led Jack to the hood of the old truck. The spaniels were already there waiting for them. Way ahead of the game as usual.

Jack looked over his shoulder to the west and south and saw two distinct lines of purple-black clouds advancing on the Workman. Both fronts were towering, dense walls of dark clouds. The leading edges were spinning and boiling and sending small vertical tornadic spikes down to the ground. He could see, even from this distance, the thick curtains of precipitation sweeping the mountains and foothills. Lightning strikes were shooting up from the ground and connecting with electric shots from the storms. The muffled sound of distant thunder rumbled across the Workman.

"Damn nasty weather coming, Elmer. I knew it when I saw the lenticulars yesterday. Those clouds always mean weather. Heat's gonna break soon."

"Up north doesn't look too damn inviting either," and both men examined a similar storm mass bearing down from up Alberta way. The temperature was now dropping towards eighty, down from a noontime reading of ninety-seven in the shade according to Elmer's large, clock-like thermometer nailed to a beam on the front porch. A cool gust of wind out of the west kicked up some red-brown dust, ruffled the dogs' curly hair and blew Jack's old, beat-up Chicago Cubs hat off his head and toward the sage flat in the east. "And holy shit. Look-it over East. There's more goddamned weather building out there. Keerist, must be a damn hurricane or something. Damn storms are coming at us from all directions. We're surrounded. Pass the goddamned whiskey."

Another blast of wind, this one smelling of cold rain and shooting up from the south, knocked over a shovel and rake over by the stockyard.

"We're in for it, buddy," said Elmer around a slug of rye. "I can sense it. This one's gonna blow everything to Kingdom Come. Maybe even put out those fires," and he pointed in the direction of the hole in the ground, the one that had swallowed a Dark Star truck and two of its men, the place where the explosion had torn the earth wide open. Smoke was still issuing from the tear in the land, and the ground for hundreds of yards all around the blast site was too hot to walk on. "Damn, I think my barbecue is about to be put on goddamned permanent hold real damn soon."

"I've never seen anything like this around here," said Jack as he stubbed out his smoke, lit another and reached for the whiskey. "Bad weather from a couple of directions, sure, but never coming in on us from all over the place. This shit's coming in fast and from everywhere."

Before Elmer could answer, gusts of cold air whipped down on them from all directions forming a miniature tornado out on the edge of the desiccated sage flat. The funnel drove straight for a metal grain bin that expanded then imploded with the rapidly fluctuating air pressure caused by the tightly spinning air. Then the corrugated structure enlarged like a

balloon and ripped apart. Thousands of kernels of
dried corn were sucked into the air looking like a
gigantic swarm of bees. From there the mini-tornado
rocked off toward Elmer's barn and flattened half of
that before bouncing and buffeting out across the
prairie headed east shooting small bolts of static
electricity in every directions, each strike sounding like
the report of a 30.06 rifle. Sage bushes, roots and all,
were sucked out of the ground and whirled to the top
of the now full-scale twister. Even from a distance of a
quarter-mile or so the shriek of the tormented air
sounded like someone was grinding an enormous ax
blade on a stone wheel. A sage bush was ejected from
the cyclone and the six-foot plant shot straight at Jack
and Elmer, who both dove to the ground an instant
before the bush smashed through the truck's window.
That sent the sixteen Boykins scurrying to the front
porch, umber eyes wide with excitement, thirty-two
ears flapping in the wind.

Elmer stood up clutching the bottle of rye and
yelled, "Damn storm's gonna son-of-a-bitchin' level my
place," and he took a huge pull of the whiskey. "Tell you
what I'm thinking. I hope every damn thing gets
flattened in this rigmarole," he bellowed. "Time to
build some new structure around here. Build a big
goddamned tower for the telescope and really give
those heavens a once over. Give me something to do.
Idle hands are the work of the devil. Know what I mean
'bout that there shit?"

"Elmer, you're crazy as hell," said Jack above the
wind that was now hammering the land from all
directions at steadily increasing beat. Fifty, sixty,
seventy mile-an-hour gusts. And lightning strikes
crashing all around them every second. The storm's
velocity and volume hurt their ears. The temperature
was in the forties now, a fifty-degree drop in twenty

minutes. High altitude cirrus clouds muted the sun before they were in turn blocked out by walls of cumulonimbus. Mammatus, mean-looking clouds resembling large breasts, quickly formed beneath the bases of the storms, pulsed to the ground and then back into the dark heart of the climatic violence. All four fronts were now within a few miles of Elmer's place. Gulf of Mexico, Pacific, Arctic and eastern Montanan. Then the morning grew darker yet and hail beginning falling in all wind-whipped directions –. Small, pea-sized stones that quickly grew to the size of golf balls and covered the ground in white. The hail clanged off the trucks and metal out buildings and banged on top of the remains of the wooden barn and smashed out the remaining windows in Elmer's home, the ones not boarded up from the coal seam explosion awhile back. When the glass shattered, the shards cascaded down on the porch and the ground or were sucked by the wind out onto the plateau.

"Elmer, I'm going back to my place to ride this out," shouted Jack as a hailstone bounced off his head. "I'll cut back along the edge of the burned land. It'll save time."

"You'll never make it, but give 'er hell for me," and Elmer lurched off to the shelter of the porch to join his dogs who were all sitting along the wall of the house well out of the line of fire. Several chunks of ice, now the size of tennis balls, slammed into his back and shoulders, but he kept going and made the porch, swearing a blue streak all the way. Jack tore open the door to his truck, fired up the engine and shifted gears as hailstones the size of grapefruits took out his windshield. He drove off with a lap full of smashed pieces of glass the shape of huge diamonds and a pair of rock-hard snowballs bouncing in his lap. In the rear view mirror he saw Elmer laughing, and talking to the

Boykins, and then with the bottle of Beam in his hand, he saw his friend pointing at something to the north, off in the direction of Jack's place. The rain came in sheets, a downpour and that was the last he saw of Elmer. The storm dominated everything now. All he could see in front of him was the hood of the truck and a few feet of muddy ruts. He drove on like a madman trusting in his familiarity with the roads to see him through.

~ ~ ~

The speedometer in the old truck said he was doing fifty. Maybe he was. More likely the wheels were spinning through the muck, melting hail and pooling rainwater. The steering wheel bucked and lurched in his hands as the front end bounced through deep ruts and across fresh washouts in the red mud that used to be the road that ran from Elmer's along the ruined sage flat then down into Mad Woman Gulch and up again to his place. He couldn't see ten feet in front of him. The rain was coming down in a wall of water. Rips of lightning illuminated the land nearby, turning the countryside into a quick-flashing series of monotone still-life images. Fleeing antelope caught in full stride. A golden eagle frozen in flight. Swaying pines stooped at odd angles to the ground.

A white-hot bolt hammered a lone juniper on the edge of the road. The small tree exploded in a cloud of blasted wood and smoke. Jack instinctively swerved to avoid the strike, running over a small up-thrust of clinker just off the road right as the lightning exploded with a deafening crash. The front end of the truck kicked into the air and then its momentum pushed the rig off into the sage, the truck flying through space and listing toward the passenger side. He clung to the wheel and braced for the impact as the truck slammed to the ground fifty feet from the road. The pickup slid on its side, grinding against rock and pushing into the saturated soil. Pieces of sagebrush, entire plants and clumps of gumbo flew into the cab. All of this happened in seconds but Jack felt as though he were watching everything in exceptionally slow motion. He watched while hanging onto the wheel with clenched fists as the truck plowed into boulders, pieces of grillwork and shattered headlights flying up over his side of the cab. Sounds of tearing metal, fragmenting glass and shearing chrome trim reached his ears above the storm's din. A spray of mud and small rock poured through the space where the windshield used to be. A splintered piece of sage embedded itself in his upper arm and his face felt like it was being mangled by shotgun pellets.

The truck stopped sliding. The rain and lightning were stronger than ever. The wind was howling, moaning like an insane beast. He could smell the steam from the truck's ruined radiator and the odor of leaking gasoline. The door on his side was crumpled shut, but the window on the driver's side was smashed out and Jack worked his way through the opening, shoving the sage out of the way. He worked his chest free, then wriggled his legs clear, falling to the mud with a wet thump. He pulled the stick from his arm and blood poured out. He tried to stand up but the wind slammed him against the drive train of the exposed undercarriage, knocking him back down. He crawled around to the front of the truck but there was no relief from the wind and rain. A series of lightning strikes to his right illuminated the tear in the earth caused by the burning coal seams. Huge jets of steam and fountains of orange-red sparks were exploding all along the rip in the plateau. The wind dropped for an instant and now he could hear the roar of the vaporizing rainfall, the bursting sound of the seams of coal that were at once exploding into sheets of fire and also being extinguished by the downpour that was like no rain he'd had ever seen. Not rain, rather an avalanche of water now along with the constant flash and afterglow of lightning and the fusillade of roaring of thunderclaps.

The wind picked up where it left off and increased in intensity. Sagebrush, Ponderosa limbs, hunks of grass, whole juniper trees, rocks blew past him in all directions as the gale swirled and ravaged the land. A tremendous gust first blew the truck on its back collapsing the cab roof, then another shrieking blast rolled the pickup in the direction of the steaming inferno. Jack was blown against a small rise of limestone, the force of the impact breaking his already wounded right arm and tearing a gash in his leg. He wrapped his good arm and legs around a rectangular piece of the rock and screamed "Go ahead you bastard. Kill me. KILL ME!" and he saw through the rain and the blood his truck roll over and over, wheels flying from the axles, frame contorting, the Ford rolling to the edge of the widening crevasse and then disappear. Seconds later the gas tank exploded. A ball of flame rose briefly above the rim of the gash before the insane rain beat down the flames.

"I'm dead. Totally dead," he yelled and thought about Elmer telling him to "give 'er hell." He renewed his grip on the rock as the wind roared around him. The air grew colder.

He held this way for eternity, becoming part of the gritty stone, until he noticed that the gale was letting up some. So was the rain. The lightning and thunder were moving back in the directions they'd originated from. The temperature was below freezing. He was cold and he thought 'That's something. Cold means I'm still alive.' The rain stopped and the wind died. He let loose of the rock, rolled away in the congealing mud. He slowly stood up and moaned when he felt the broken bone in his arm. He looked around. All he could see was the nearby sage flat swept clean of all plants and surrounding trees. The land had been scoured to a lifeless, barren landscape. The storm had sucked water from the small ponds and little creeks. He could see the funnels of steam rising from the rent in the ground but no more flames or sparks. The land was dead still. Dark purple and black clouds swirled and boiled soundlessly only a few hundred feet above him. It was now so cold that the puddles of water had ice on their edges and the mud was almost hard. The hard taste of snow tinged the air. All was silent except for the distant-sounding hiss of steam.

"WAHHHOOOARRERRR..."

The sound tore across the land and through Jack. He looked over to where the flat dropped into Mad Woman Gulch.

The wolf was standing there staring at him. Huge. Three-hundred pounds. Nearly four-feet tall at the shoulder. Massive head. Jaws filled with large, menacing teeth that glistened bone white. Deep-yellow eyes glowed in the dim light. The animal moved several paces nearer him and roared again.

"WAHHHOOOARRERRR..."

The howl froze Jack. A sound from another time. Wild. Primitive. Ancient.

The wolf stood motionless and the two creatures, man and wolf, looked at each other over the distance of time. The wolf's eyes glowed even more brightly and beams of light from the animal's soul seemed to burn into Jack. All he could see was a brilliant band of white light like an electric river flowing from his mind to join the larger current that was the wolf. The streams merged and Jack ceased being Jack. He was the wolf

killing the mastiffs then loping across the high plains
in the night. He was his father watching the enormous
cat leaping over him in that Sierra Madre Occidental
canyon so long ago. He was Natalie screwing Foxen. He
was Elmer hopping up and down smoking a cigar and
drinking the rye whiskey as he and the sixteen Boykins
cavorted around the storm-leveled remains of his
ranch house. He was all of those at Wimp's funeral
alongside the road decades ago and he smelled the
antelope cooking and sizzling over the fire and he heard
Coaker playing his fiddle and everyone laughing. And
then he was the Workman. He flowed through the river
canyon and up his little stream. He was liquid and he
was the layers of coal, slate and sandstone. He saw the
forever vastness of the plateau from the high limbs of
Ponderosa. He felt the wind glide through the trees'
long needles. And he watched as countless rattlesnakes
and milk snakes and gopher snakes poured from
openings in the piles of sandstone and from holes in the
ground beneath the sage. And he smelled the pungent
sweetness of those plants. The hiss and rattle of the
snakes became him. The rock, the animals, the
subterranean rivers flowing under the forest of
Ponderosa and the barren sage flats, he was all of this
and the wind sailing through everywhere, and he saw
far beyond Mad Woman Gulch to the view from the
summit of Chambers Point. He saw the solid land
flowing eternally with complex rhythms, drifting
through eons, rising and falling and reforming again,
and he watched forests come and go, and rock cliffs
carved by the wind crumble to stone and dust and he
watched a land that was simultaneously glowing under
a radiant sun and a star-packed night sky, and a huge
moon perpetually rose and fell pouring silver light over
the Workman. The Northern Lights. Meteors. St.
Elmo's Fire. He watched all of this over time because

he was the land and he saw the wolf looking into him and saying with a voice that knew no language "All of this. All of us. One. The land." And he stepped through the writhing and coiling rings of snakes and walked towards the edge of the cliff on the northern edge of Chambers Point where he watched Jupiter, a gigantic, swirling mass of colorful gases rising above the bluffs. And now he walked through a million years of the softly falling snow and stepped off the cliff trusting in the river of blue-white light...

-The End-

Thank you for reading.
Please review this book. Reviews help others find Absolutely Amazing eBooks and inspire us to keep providing these marvelous tales.

If you would like to be put on our email list to receive updates on new releases, contests, and promotions, please go to AbsolutelyAmazingEbooks.com and sign up.

ABOUT THE AUTHOR

John Holt is the author of over two dozen published books including *Plain Crazy in Paradise, Blown Away Under the Big Sky, The Lost Patrol, Yellowstone Drift – Floating the Past in Real Time, Arctic Aurora – Canada's Yukon and Northwest Territories, Coyote Nowhere – In Search of America's Last Frontier*. His work has appeared in such publications as *Men's Journal, Fly Fisherman, High Country News, Crossroads, E – The Environmental Magazine*, and *Gray's Sporting Journal*. He and his wife, photographer Ginny, live in Livingston, Montana.

ABSOLUTELY AMA⚡ING eBOOKS

AbsolutelyAmazingEbooks.com

or AA-eBooks.com